THE TREK CREW BOOK

By James Van Hise

PIONEER BOOKS   **LAS VEGAS, NEVADA**

Designed and edited by Hal Schuster

Library of Congress Cataloging-in-Publication Data
Van Hise, James,   1949—
    The Trek Crew Book

    1. Star Trek (Television program) I. Title
ISBN 1-55698-

International Standard Book Number: 1-55698-

First Printing 1989

CONTENTS

1991 will mark the silver anniversary of **Star Trek**; twenty-five years in the hearts and minds of its fans. Even though a second television series sends **The Next Generation** going boldly where no one has gone before, it remains the original **Star Trek** which continues to capture the enthusiasm of the most fans. The old show is even referred to by many as "Trek Classic" to differentiate it from what is being filmed today.

These pages chronicle the performers, as well as the characters they played, and perhaps in all this can be found a key to the elusive magic others have tried to capture since. Leonard Nimoy has referred to the process as trying to capture "lightning in a bottle." If it can be done at all, it happens only rarely, and then under circumstances virtually impossible to repeat.

Even if the original cast of **Star Trek** does not continue to make feature films the way they did from 1979through '89, it will be the standard they set, in the Sixties, Seventies and Eighties, by which other efforts will continue to be measured. As much as newcomers may continue to try to capture "lightning in a bottle," its the energy and the electricity in those original episodes of the Sixties that will continue to inspire and impress viewers decades from now. All the while, people will continue to wonder just what keeps them so fresh and alive decades after they were filmed. Perhaps it's the characters. Perhaps it's the performers. Perhaps it's a magical combination of both. All we do know is that the **Star Trek** crew we came to know in the Sixties is the one that continues to come to mind whenever the words STAR TREK are heard.

—JAMES VAN HISE

October 29, 1989

INTRO....

THE CAPTAIN

Report by Scott Nance and Jay Wilson

Commander Thomas Kirk considered it lucky that he got his weeklong pass from Starfleet to be back home in Iowa when his wife, Martha, delivered their son, James.

Within six months of James' birth, Tom's tour as first officer aboard the frigate *Quicksilver* ended, and he was able to manage to get an administration position at Spacedock orbiting the Earth. Tom was able to commute home by shuttle and be a "regular father" to little Jimmy.

Of course, like all Starfleet fathers, Tom loved to tell his space stories to his son. And within a year and a half, Martha gave birth to the Kirks' second child, George, who would later in life prefer to be called "Sam." Tom loved to have his two sons on his knees to tell these strange and exotic tales to.

Jim and Sam were close as children, although from an early age, they were quite different. Jim was the one who received the advanced swimming certificate at age nine, while Sam was the one who won the science fair three years in a row. Jim was athletic, outgoing and adventurous, while Sam was quiet and interested in school work. But these differences only served to unite the brothers as they helped each other with their own weaknesses.

Jim made average grades as the years went by at school. He was well-liked and particularly popular with the girls. It was Diane, Jean, Wendy, Anne, all in one week's time. And then the following week he'd start all over with new ones. Jim played the field quite a bit, and if it wasn't for his youth, he might've been accused of using his women.

At the age of 14, Jim joined the Starfleet Junior Leadership Corps. Entrance was difficult, but it provided motivation to keep his grades up. The corps maintained rigid standards of academics, physical ability and honor. Once he had begun mastering his school work, Jim was a natural for the Juniors.

His popularity quickly led him to command of the local regiment. Jim's natural physical ability was supplemented by the discipline of the corps. He had to fine-tune his practical skills running obstacle courses and in hand-to-hand combat. Jim undertook demanding workout programs to keep himself at his peak. In high school, he ran for the track team.

The Juniors met regularly and engaged in maneuvers throughout Iowa. The group, which included about two dozen kids, went on mock planetary encounters, and travelled to Starfleet installations on Earth and once even to the orbiting monolithic Spacedock.

Jim's first time in space was on the shuttle ride to that field trip to Spacedock. Space swallowed Jim Kirk like a wave. He just stared into the depths of space, soaking in the abundance of stars. He could not tear his eyes away from the

PROFILE

front viewers. The depth made Jim dizzy, and this dizziness created a greater sense of wonder in the boy.

Sometimes the activities would cause Jim stress. He had to lead the regular formal corps meetings, keep himself primed physically, and maintain good grades. Finally, Tom Kirk became the local Juniors' new adult advisor. That gave Jim a reason to push even harder: to make his father proud. At times, it seemed to Jim that his life was an inescapable whirlpool.

That's when Jim and a couple of close friends, also from the Juniors, began to go on monorail trips to New York City, Los Angeles, Chicago, Toronto, Melbourne, L ondon and elsewhere. Despite working in space, the Kirks had always been a little provincial, staying close to their Iowa roots. Now Jim was breaking out on his own, unknown to his parents.

Although he had studied contemporary culture in school, meeting it nose-to-nose gave Jim a surrealistic feeling, like he was in a movie, but that's exactly what pushed him. Jim wanted to see more, do more; he wanted to explore.

These little secret jaunts did him good. It was his leisure amidst duty. Jim continued to lean on his brother Sam for help with school, and in turn, Jim began taking Sam on these excursions. Sam was also curious, but didn't take the chances, the adventures that Jim placed himself in while in the cities. Jim needed risk, but Sam was cautious.

By the time Jim was 17, he had moved up to Honorary Cadet Status in the Juniors, which of course made Tom Kirk proud. Tom was sympathetic to Jim's pressures, but he could also see these pressures shaping his son to command action later in life.

Martha Kirk had returned to work as a design supervisor in the private sector. She dealt with civilians, and heard all of the civilians' stories of their children: boys, girls, sports teams, shopping and more boys and more girls. For her, it seemed a saner existence for her children than military maneuvers and trials out on the phaser range. She continued to worry about Jim, although she knew she had lost him to the glamour and excitement of Starfleet.

She was heartened when Sam, her other son, announced he was applying to college—as a civilian—with a major in biology.

At the age of 16, Sam began to apply for early acceptance to several prestigious Earth and off-world universities, including the Vulcan Science Academy, which he finally chose to attend. His big brother Jim was very proud of him, but Jim already had his hands full, eyeing an acceptance into Starfleet Academy.

Late in the spring of his last year in high school, Jim and his father travelled to San Francisco, where Starfleet Academy itself was located. There was a day of extensive and intensive tests, which pushed Jim to his limits. The tests were mostly academic in nature, rather than physical fitness, which frustrated him. He had to recall everything he had ever heard Sam discuss! Jim passed, but without much margin for safety.

Jim's near-fail scared him. *I almost didn't make it,* he thought. He buckled down and prepared for entrance into the next semester in the Academy by reviewing with Sam all summer. Jim vowed to leave the frivolity behind him. Starfleet was no place for that. And a commission meant more to Jim Kirk than a good time did.

He was one of the first to arrive at Starfleet Academy in the fall. He had been to San Francisco before on his monorail trips, so he was able to handle himself until the dorms opened two weeks after his arrival. When dorm assignments were made, Jim found himself bunking with a cadet named Gary Mitchell.

Gary was a smart-alecky, carefree, fun-loving young man, which disturbed Jim's new academic resolve occasionally, but they soon became good friends. As classes began, Jim pushed himself harder than anyone else. He stood straighter and his uniform was cleaner than anyone else's and he strived to be the best. Jim worked until he began making his classmates look bad.

One cadet, Finnegan, took offense. He didn't enjoy being second best. He decided he'd loosen up Cadet Kirk personally. Finnegan wrecked Jim's phasers, ripped Jim's uniforms and once even adjusted the sonic shower so that it disrupted Jim's brain so as to make it appear Jim was drunk one time during morning class. But Jim never broke his resolve, and he considered it a moral victory even though Finnegan continued to terrorize Cadet Kirk. Fortunately for Jim, Finnegan dropped out after one year. Jim's resolve, however, enabled him to make it to sophomore year. But Finnegan had shaken him, and Jim would always jump whenever he heard the name Finnegan.

The rest of his Academy days were relatively easy-going compared to that tension headache of a first year with Finnegan. Jim and Gary Mitchell went out, partied, and by the time Jim was an upperclassman, he had loosened up quite a bit. He had won great praise from his teachers, especially those in the military sciences. Jim gained confidence in his future in Starfleet.

Tom, Martha, and Sam—who was on leave from the Vulcan Academy—were all able to make it to the West Coast for the graduation ceremony. Then Jim entered the year-long Command School. Command School, with its military structure and emphasis on martial arts rather than liberal arts, was a breeze for Jim. It reminded him of the Junior Corps. It was during Command School that he was required to read the autobiographical works of Garth of Izar. Garth was perhaps the most brilliant commander of the time and became Jim's role model.

Jim didn't like to lose. He had never lost: he made it into the Academy, Finnegan flunked out before too much damage could be done; throughout life, Jim didn't lose. He always found someone or something to help him win. Therefore, he wasn't too keen on the *Kobayashi Maru* no-win scenario. The night before the test, Jim and Gary snuck into the main computer center and spent the entire night reprogramming the simulator so the deflectors and warp drive wouldn't fail during his run.

And so Jim pulled his command back from the Neutral Zone in one piece. The admiral running the test was dumbfounded, to say the least. Later that night, over a bottle of Saurian brandy, Jim was bragging about his feat. But also in the lounge, unknown to Jim, was that same Academy admiral, who after hearing this tale, brought Kirk before a review board. Instead of bucking this cadet, the board officially commended him for original thinking. Kirk was the right combination of skill and brass, and it was pure talent.

Jim's love life also improved. For the past couple years he had allowed himself more leisure time than during the early Academy days, and he was pleased to find that he had never lost his touch with the ladies. The women, his friendship with the easygoing, laid-back Mitchell, and the promise of an excellent career, gave Jim confidence to go out and become a leader.

Aboard the *USS Farragut*, Jim finally found himself in space on active duty, his dream since before entering the Juniors. While Garth was a man of flair and theatrics in his strategies, Captain Garrovick was cautious and plodding. Although Jim found Garth's techniques more exciting, he saw that his captain's methods were proven and brought the same results with less risk to the crew.

Kirk was manning the phaser station belowdecks when the Farragut encountered the Cloud Thing from Tycho IV. The Cloud was upon the Federation ship quickly, and young Kirk, now an ensign but still quite green, was startled. It was his first true space battle. Jim hesitated—only for a second—before firing the phaser shots that drove the creature away. The melee had left more than half the crew dead, and for many years, Kirk would blame those deaths on his own hesitation.

Starfleet Command was of a different mind. For his efforts in battle, Jim was commended. The *Farragut* limped along with a skeleton crew to Starbase 15 for an extended drydock and repair. That ship would be out of service for nearly a year, so the entire remaining crew was reassigned. This action ended Jim's cadet cruise three months early.

He continued to blame himself for the deaths. It had been horrible. The thing had drained the red corpuscles from hundreds of men and women. Because of that creature, Kirk felt space was no longer opening up for him. He felt space was pushing him back. He felt unwelcome. Jim Kirk chose to return to the Academy on Earth as an instructor in military science.

Jim pushed his cadets hard. He wanted to instill in them the same resolve and dedication to an Academy education that he had had. He didn't want any of his students to flunk, and sometimes acted the tyrant to his class. Gary Mitchell ended up taking advance classes under Jim. "In Lieutenant Kirk's class, you think or you sink," they said. Yes, Jim was a full lieutenant by this time.

Gary had been having a devil of a time in his old friend Jim's class. And he needed to pass this extra class if he wanted a promotion from lieutenant, junior grade, to full lieutenant. The carefree, mischievous Mitchell—rather than studying—created an elaborate plan to peacefully remove Kirk from the scene. Gary set up Jim with a young lady named Ruth. Within two months, Jim and Ruth had fallen in love. Ruth was peaceful, serene, gentle. She was a calming force in Jim's life in contrast to the active military. They decided to marry. Kirk requested and received a two-week pass.

Ruth and Jim decided that only a few months weren't enough to base years' worth of commitment on. They remained seriously involved, but without forcing a commitment. Ruth and Jim enjoyed their two weeks alone, away from the regimen and discipline of Starfleet. Back at the Academy, Gary was able to hustle the substitute instructor quite easily, and he passed Jim's class with flying colors.

At the end of the year, Jim's trauma faded. He once again was anxious for space. *Enough sitting around like an old stuffed shirt, moping,* Jim thought. He transferred over as first officer of the *USS Constitution* for a five year mission. Jim demonstrated his brilliance again and again in landing missions. Skill and bravery, skill and bravery. He never missed a beat. Starfleet was beginning to realize what they had on their hands.

At the age of 33, Kirk leapt from lieutenant commander to captain. He was named commander of the *Enterprise,* which would be undertaking the most intense five-year mission ever attempted. Only the top two percent of any Starfleet Academy-graduated class would be allowed to serve aboard her. And with the help of a Vulcan named Spock and a doctor named McCoy, Jim Kirk would never lose.

Although Jim was rotated back to Earth at the end of his first five-year mission, he'd regain command of the refitted *Enterprise,* a ship which he would eventually lose on the same day he lost his son. But Kirk never allowed adversities that cripple lesser men to hold him back. With a new *Enterprise* under his command, Kirk would continue to prove that he was still *the* Starfleet officer to be reckoned with.

A Canadian by birth, Shatner's interest in the theatre was established at an early age. He was appearing in plays at the age of 12, but it wasn't until he was planning for college that he made it clear to his parents that he wanted to study acting. This came as a particular blow to his father, who expected his son to train to take over the family business. The compromise he reached with his family was that he would study economics at McGill University while also exploring the wonders of the theatre department.

Upon graduating from McGill, he went to work as a business manager for an acting company. But he wasn't very good at that and they finally chose to hire him on as a member of the performing company. He had been accepted as an actor by fellow actors, however modest the company. This led to an invitation to join the then just forming Stratford, Ontario repertory company. It was there that he captured the attention of the prestigious theatre director Tyrone Guthrie, who took the young Shatner under his wing as his protege. For three years the young actor played in the works of Shakespeare and that of other classic writers of the stage alongside such illustrious performers as James Mason, Anthony Quayle and Sir Alec Guinness.

At the age of 25, Shatner won the Tyrone Guthrie Stratford Festival Scholarship and used it to move to New York City and launch himself on the next stage of his career. So in 1956 he arrived in New York in a Stratford production of "Tamburlaine" which received excellent notices and folded after only twenty performances. But he used the opportunity to pursue work on the New York stage and in television. In the Fifties a great deal of TV production originated in New York and Shatner took instant advantage of that, managing to land one role after another without having to spend years pounding the pavement or trying to prove himself with the sporadic roles young actors tend to find.

The day after "Tamburlaine" folded, Shatner was offered a seven year contract by Twentieth Century Fox which would begin at $500 a week, about ten times what he was earning in the theatre. But he took someone's advice and turned it down. Things kept happening for him, though, as he landed the role of one of the principals in the 1958 MGM release **The Brothers Karamazov**, which caused MGM to offer Shatner a non-exclusive two picture deal at $50,000 per film. While Shatner signed the contract, he later decided to get out of it when he read for the male lead in a new play, "The World of Suzie Wong." Since appearing in a play with daily performances, movie work would be out. Getting a new agent when his current one wouldn't help him get out of the MGM contract, the studio was only too happy to comply. It was a "pay or play" contract which lasted one year and would pay the actor $100,000 whether the studio had films for him to appear in or not, and since MGM was going through a slump that year, they knew they wouldn't have any projects for him. They were only too happy to tear up the contract and save some money.

The play opened in October, 1958 to largely bad notices. The script Shatner had read and found so exciting had been cut and altered until by opening night it bore little resemblance to what he had signed on for. But the show had a million dollar advance in ticket sales before it opened in New York and so was

THE ACTOR

insured a minimum three month run. During that time Shatner used every acting trick he knew to alter the pace and make the play more lively. What had been transmogrified into a turgid drama, Shatner began to play as a comedy. While initially entire rows of people had been getting up and walking out, this began to occur with less and less frequency. Finally the play became a hit! It ran for two years, won Drama Circle acting awards, and Shatner won the Theatre Guild Award as Best Actor of the Year. Shatner followed that up with a one-year run in "A Shot In The Dark" paying opposite Walter Matthau.

In television of the time Shatner also garnered positive notices. For his performance with Lee J. Cobb in Arthur Hailey's "No Deadly Medicine" on **Studio One**, both *Variety* and *New York Daily News* had nothing but superlatives for the young actor. He brought the role of a young successor to a once-great aging physician grown careless in his old age to life. Shatner's work on **The U.S. Steel Hour** and **Playhouse 90** received equally high critical marks.

One of Shatner's early high points on dramatic TV occurred in a script by Rod Serling for **Playhouse 90** on June 19, 1958. In "A Town Has Turned To Dust," Shatner co-stars with Rod Steiger in a decidedly non-heroic role which received the following review by Jack Gould in the *New York Times* for June 20, 1958: "Mr. Shatner gave one of the best performances of his career. As the town bully and ringleader of the lynching party, he was the embodiment of hate and blind physical passion. Mr. Shatner's attention to detail in putting together the picture of an ignorant and evil social force was remarkable. . . Two of the season's superlative performances by Rod Steiger and William Shatner."

In spite of these fine critical notices, Shatner was passed over for the movie version of **The World of Suzie Wong**, the role he established on stage going to William Holden in 1960. This would not be the last time he would lose a role to another actor after first establishing the part. An early role Shatner won acclaim for was as the son in the father-son legal team in "The Defenders" which was broadcast on **Studio One** in 1957. When **The Defenders** was picked up for series in 1961, the role Shatner essayed four years earlier went to Robert Reed, while the role of the elder partner was recast from Ralph Bellamy to E.G. Marshall. But Shatner turned down the lead in **Dr. Kildare**, a show which went on to run for five years and was even more successful than **The Defenders**.

In 1961, Shatner appeared in two important films of the time. In **The Intruder** he plays a rabble-rouser who travels from one Southern town to another, inciting people to riot against court-ordered school integration. It's a film which is just as timely now as it was 27 years ago. It was subsequently re-released under the titles **I Hate Your Guts!** and **Shame**. Shatner also appears in **Judgment at Nuremburg**, the Stanley Kramer directed film which garnered a great deal of attention and comment at the time of its release. Shatner is relegated to a bit part as a liaison for one of the three judges, but he was nevertheless in the company of such stalwart screen performers as Spencer Tracy, Burt Lancaster, Richard Widmark, Marlene Dietrich, Judy Garland, Maximil

ian Schell, and Montgomery Clift. Not many actors can say they worked with performers of that stature, much less all in the same film!

In 1965, Shatner agreed to star in a TV pilot for a show called **Star Trek**. Had the series not sold, Shatner would have seriously considered retiring from acting. Even though he states that he would have considered "selling ties in Macy's," he more likely would have pursued writing and directing work, something that he already had some small experience in. But the series did sell and brought Shatner enduring popularity at the cost of his marriage. In an interview appearing June 22, 1968, Shatner told *TV Guide* he may have lost his marriage and sold out his dreams of becoming a movie star by pursuing the immediate financial security of TV work. With the damage to his private life, he found that his long sought-after success was "empty." When a dream dies, he says, "there's such a terrible void, such a loss. I find myself clinging to times when life was a joy, a thing to cherish. Today, I'd characterize success as security and love." Working six days a week, ten to fourteen hours a day, wrecked havoc with his family life. By the time the series was dropped, Shatner's marriage had also been cancelled and the divorce settlement wiped him out financially. In certain respects it was back to square one. He no longer had a financial cushion which would enable him to pick and choose roles, and wound up taking almost anything which paid well. It was during this period that he performed in such films as the Spanish-made **White Comanche**. While he also made respectable guest appearances on TV series, none were comparable to the Golden Age of television drama he had performed in the late Fifties. Films such as **Sole Survivor** in 1969 cast Shatner playing second fiddle to former Ben Casey Vincent Edwards. Numerous game shows, state fairs and other appearances supplemented his TV work. His nadir during this period must be the film **Impulse** made in Florida in 1974. The biggest expense in this independent production was Shatner's salary as the script is strictly from hunger. He plays a character who kills his shrewish wife and then stalks a little girl whom he suspects has evidence against him. The director allowed Shatner to run amuck on camera and overact shamelessly. Other actors, such as the late Harold Sakata (Oddjob in **Goldfinger**) are equally misused in this trite waste of celluloid.

That Shatner could continue to turn out fine work the proper opportunity and direction was demonstrated in 1970 in the **Hollywood Television Theatre** production of "The Andersonville Trial." The producer felt he owed Shatner a kindness for something the actor had done for him once years before and chose to repay Shatner by offering him the lead in this complex courtroom drama. Shatner played a military officer just after the close of the Civil War who was prosecuting the commandant of a prisoner of war camp in the South. Shatner's adversary is played by Richard Basehart, a fine actor whom he had worked with just the year before in **Sole Survivor**. Not since **Star Trek** had Shatner so dominated the screen in a performance. His sharp questioning of Basehart and his ascerbic, bitter responses formed the linchpin of this drama which explores both the underlying conflicts of the Civil War and many of the themes tackled in **Judgment at Nuremburg**. Shot to video rather than film, its theme of the breakdown of human decency and the sacrifices made during wartime is an eternal one. It remains one of Shatner's finest performances as it is explosive when the material demands without straying into ham-fisted delivery. It hearkens back to his earlier dramatic television work. The production as a whole captures the essence of those classic teleplays from **Playhouse 90, Studio One, Kraft Theatre** and **The U.S. Steel Hour** and so many other fine productions from the 1950s.

It was during the production of "The Andersonville Trial" that Shatner met Marcy Lafferty, who would become his second wife. He credits her support with helping him endure the trials and tribulations of this stage of his career.

Shatner continued his roller-coaster career achieving highs and plunging to lows throughout the Seventies as he took jobs which paid well while continuing to pursue more prestigious roles. One such was his starring performance in the 1976 telefilm **The Tenth Level**. But this period also saw less than memorable roles in such films as **The Devil's Rain** and **Big Bad Mama** (which contains Shatner's only celluloid nude scene).

In 1978 the long rumored, on-again, off-again, **Star Trek** finally came to the screen as a motion picture rather than a TV series, which Shatner had at one point been signed for. It was released on December 7, 1979 and scored big at the boxoffice, although its $40 million budget prevented there being much of a profit. The scaled-down budgets of the subsequent three films enabled their average $70 to $80 million U.S. grosses to be very profitable. Only **Star Trek V**, which Shatner directed himself, proved disappointing, grossing only $50 million domestically. Although received with mixed results by both fans and critics, it was not a bad film, just an overly predictable one. Shatner's directing was more than adequate.

Shatner has obviously come to regard Captain Kirk as more than just one of the many roles he has played over the years. In fact, it is undoubtedly the pivotal role of his career as it first enabled him to achieve popular recognition, and then ten years after last playing the role it revitalized his career once more.

His renewed, widespread popularity was ably demonstrated in 1982 when he starred in **T.J. Hooker**, a rather commonplace police action series which lasted four years solely on the strength of Shatner's popularity.

Regarding his role as Captain Kirk, In his autobiography, **Shatner: Where No Man. . .** (Tempo Books, 1979), he is quoted as saying, "I tried always to play Kirk close to myself—in the way that I would have wanted to behave if I were in that situation, as if it were real. I played Kirk as I was, and as I would have hoped to be.

"I will play Kirk again as I always have, close to myself. I have grown and he will have grown.

"I'll strive for even more emotional openness, more depth, more subtlety, more communication, more love. I've learned—that's really what life is all about."

Why does William Shatner, for over fifteen years the captain of the *Starship Enterprise* hate "The Trouble With Tribbles?" He explains, "I don't like Tribbles. The whole answer starts at some college in Connecticut. There I was, acting my little heart out. I'm in a scene, saying something or other and then. . . THUNK! A tribble!

Let me hastily add, for those of you with tribble in hand, don't get any ideas.

There was a bright spotlight on me, and I just saw something white go by, and suddenly my mind went back to one convention I had been at in New York where somebody threw something at me — it was a pie. But it was a week-old pie! It could have been used as a tire! At the last instant, as it was coming toward me, I'd seen this thing coming at me, and ARRGH! 'Whack!' It hit me on the shoulder — and this guy raced out before me, as five thousand people jumped on him — they all wanted to protect their Captain, you know. Imagine, five thousand Trekkies suddenly become an enraged mob!

"First of all, in that instant that that thing came by, I didn't know what it was. I gotta tell you, pie didn't really enter my mind as it went sailing by! Then the guards jumped on this guy, so I said to the crowd, 'All right!! Let's find out why he did that! Stand away, stand back.' You know, the whole psychological bit!! All I could think of throughout was, my God, it's happening again!

What that taught me was not to talk too much to college audiences."

Shatner's thoughts returned to **Star Trek**, "We made it about six days per segment. So anything that's complicated, about what's going on inside is avoided. So, **Star Trek**— there I am faced time and again with challenges that I, as an actor, had never been faced with. Then one day a script comes in and it says, 'a woman comes into your body.' I point to that show to serve as an example of the challenges I was faced with!"

William Shatner performed years of live stage before moving to Hollywood to launch his movie and television career. But what type of training did he receive before entering theatre? "I really never did do the slightest formal study, but what I did was devote a lot of years to acting. I started when I was a kid, about six years old. I did a play at some camp in the northern wilds of Quebec. I think they sent me up there to get rid of me. All I remember was people were trying to take me away from my dog. I always wanted one, and my parents' argument was, in the muddy streets of Montreal, the dog would run around outside, come in, and dirty the carpets and furniture. They'd say, 'You can have a hobby horse — but you can't have a dog!' So now that I'm an adult — I've really got dogs, I breed them — Dobermans — and so I remember my crying on stage as a kid, 'Don't take my dog away from me!!!' And the audience of parents was crying — but whether it was my acting that made the audience cry, or something that they saw in the performance, didn't matter. I felt that I had touched the crowd, at the age of six."

Besides the obvious strains of a high pressure acting career, there is also the risk of personal injury in roles that involve a great deal of on-screen action. Although stunt men do shield actors from the worst hazards it is not uncom-

INTERVIEW

mon for them to suffer injury. "See, my finger's all bent out of shape," Shatner laments. "I also broke my leg. But I'll tell you about my finger. The finger was sort of after **Star Trek**, but I blame it on **Star Trek** because I was Captain Kirk!

"Do you know who Harold Sakata is? He was Odd Job in **Goldfinger**. He's a professional wrestler. His neck muscles came out of his ears. He's 250 pounds, and a beautiful Hawaiian man. He's built like your average alien.

"So I'm standing on top of a roof, and I'm supposed to throw this lariat over — and land it over his head, then pull him up, tie it down, and run around the side of the building. This movie was so low-budget that the director gave me this line to say, 'Hang in there!'

*(Editor's Note: the low-budget film he's talking about is a forgettable effort called **Impulse**)*

So I said to the director, 'I can jump off that roof and slide down the rope!' And so he said, 'You can do that?' 'Hey man, I'm Captain Kirk!' was my swift reply. But this movie was so low-budget, that when I say lariat, I don't mean hemp, I mean nylon! They went out and bought clothesline.

"So I threw the lariat over Harold's head. He's got tied to him a leather-like strap, which is attached to a cable. Behind me, on the roof, are three special effects men who pull him up on the cable (out of the way of the cameras). This way, his weight is supported on his shoulders instead of his neck!

Also, I said, 'When I slide down, how can I prevent myself from slipping?' So the special effects men said they'd tie knots in the rope so I could get a hand-hold on the rope when I slide down it. Everything was working out great!

So Harold Sakata's standing below, I'm on the roof and the director yells for action. Harold Sakata's standing on boxes; the cable is attached; I throw the lariat over his head; the prop men kick away the boxes; and there he is dangling from it. And now, I slide down the rope! Suddenly, I feel my finger go CRACK! and I yell, 'AAARGHHH!'so I jumped down, looked up, and there he was. Harold Sakata, 14 feet off the ground!!! President Nixon once said, 'Let him hang there, and twist slowly in the wind.' Had he said that years ago, I would have known that a man hanging there twists and turns in the wind! So as I slid down the rope, Harold Sakata spun around with the rope! And when I got down, I looked up and saw him hanging there going 'ANNGGGGHHH-HUUUUURRRRRGGGGG-HHHHH!!' He was choking. Hanging there, he looked like a punching bag, so I gave him a nice one right into his chest. You know, I began to jab at him. Instead of that crazy line, 'Hang in there, baby,' I started yelling, 'Take this!' He just hung there going 'AAAARRRNNNNGH' — So I'm looking at this Hawaiian wrestler, thinking, 'What an incredible actor! He really looks like he's choking!' For about 10 or 15 seconds I'm jabbing away at him until suddenly it dawned on me — that guy is really choking! What he was yelling was, 'Get me down!' So I grabbed him, and then cut him down. So dear Harold figures he owes me his life — but he's got a size 14 neck now!"

Captain Kirk is known for liking his women, but which did he like best? Shatner says, "It was hard to choose between them and I really can't remember them! No, not really, but it was so long ago! It's a strange thing, but I can memorize lines very quickly and easily forget them. In fact, I can see a **Star Trek** episode today and wonder how it's going to turn out. What's going to happen next? That's the truth. On certain segments, I have no idea how it's gonna end, and I have a great time just watching them."

"Leonard spent about an hour and a half in makeup every day for months and months each year. Finally, in the third year, he ended up with scars on the backs of his ears," Shatner reveals as one of the more unusual hazards of the acting profession. "He might not have gone on to a fourth year, just because of that, had it gone to a fourth year."

Star Trek enjoyed a huge fan following yet it was cancelled, after being saved for its last season by a massive letter-writing campaign. Shatner explains why it left the air, "Essentially why every show is taken off the air. The Nielsens indicated that only a certain number of people were watching. In that third year, we were on late Friday. That's a death slot. Nobody watches television then. They don't tune in at ten, just to see a show, unless you're stoned out of your head, where you can't even find the channel selector. So the Nielsens indicated we were in the middle 40s in popularity, kind of 'never never land' since the networks figure the more popular a show is, the more they can charge for commercials. So, around the 40 to 50 area they're more likely to replace you with the hope they'll get a winner, but if they don't get a winner, they won't do much worse than in the 40s.

Filming a television series often leads to amusing mishaps that never make it to the screen. **Star Trek** is famous for its blooper reels. "The blooper film was put together for a Christmas party. It was a whole 20-minute film spliced together for the cast. We laughed and laughed at it! But as far as we were concerned, that Christmas party was the end of bloopers — 'til one day, about five years ago, I was skiing and fell. Now, I tried to get up in six feet of powder, and I'm all alone — the wind is blowing. So I felt that I would freeze. But suddenly, down the hill, I see somebody coming. He comes next to me and looks at me. Then he says, 'Have you seen the blooper film?' I said, 'What? The blooper film? Help me up for God's sake!' So that's the first time I knew the blooper film was going around the theaters. They were charging people admission to see me looking like a fool.

"You know those doors on the bridge that opened when we walked through them? Well, I don't want to destroy your fantasies, but there were two little guys behind opening the doors when we walked through them. That's right, promise.

Now, the stage hands were notorious for getting drunk, so the blooper film has a number of scenes with me bumping into the doors.

"Then, the blooper film also has an euphemism for the word shoot all through it. I said a lot of shoots! Whenever anything went wrong, I'd say, 'Shhoot!' I mean, there were many variations. Sometimes, 'Shooot!' or 'SHHHHEEEEEOOOOOOOT!' So they cut together about 25, and it sounded like, 'Shoot! Shooot! Shoot! Shoot! SHHHEEOOOOOT!'"

Watching episodes of **Star Trek**, one obvious question comes to mind. Just how many aliens did Captain Kirk really kill? "First of all, my directive from the admiralty was not to kill anybody," Shatner claims. "So, what we did was to put our phasers on 'stun.' Invariably what we did is stun the aliens. If we put it on heavy stun, they'd stay out for a while, and then we had a special device on that gun. We would open their minds so that the bad aliens would become good aliens. So I never really killed anybody. But I stunned an awful lot. Captain Kirk wasn't allowed to kill people."

Both Nimoy and Shatner have often complained about their contracts with Paramount for the television series. When they signed they never envisioned the lasting popularity of the show or the massive merchandising that would be based on their visages. "We didn't get any money from that! I'll tell you how I feel about it; how both Leonard and I feel about it.

Leonard was walking in London, England. He stopped to look at a billboard. The billboard's divided into three sections. The first section is Leonard's face with the ears — Spock — the ears are drooping. The second section has Leonard, with the drooping ears, holding a tankard of ale. The third section has an empty tankard of ale, and Leonard's face, with pointed ears straight up in the air.

"So Leonard and I had this battle with whoever licensed **Star Trek** for a long time. I mean, kids are walking around with my face on their shirts. Occasionally, I see a postcard with my face on it. People were exploiting us. So anyway, Leonard goes back to the studio and says, 'There's a demeaning billboard of me out there. Did you guys okay it?' So he goes to his lawyers and tries to sue." Nimoy and Shatner did ultimately resolve their differences with Paramount.

Sometimes it seems the actors are the last to hear. Shatner explains how he learned **Star Trek** was to be revived as a series of films. "Well, I was working on the series **Barbary Coast**, which was done at Paramount, coincidentally. It was on one end of Paramount, and **Star Trek** had been filmed at the other end of Paramount. I had never, for the longest time, revisited the stage area where **Star Trek** was filmed. So one day, I decided to go there. I was looking at the stages, y'know, for nostalgia and the good times we had there, and I walked down a row of offices, on that very cold and dismal day. They were the writer's offices for **Star Trek**. So as I'd been walking and remembering the times , I suddenly heard the sound of a typewriter! That was the strangest thing 'cause these offices were deserted. So I followed the sound. It was getting louder as I went into the building. I went down a hallway, where the offices for **Star Trek** were located, and the typewriter noise was getting louder, until finally I came to the **Star Trek** offices, and the name was still there. It read Star Tre — the 'k' was faded! I slowly opened the door and there was Gene Roddenberry! He was sitting in a corner, typing. I said, 'Gene, the series has been cancelled!' He said, 'I know, I know the series has been cancelled! I'm writing the movie!' So I said, 'There's going to be a movie? What's it gonna be about?' So he says, 'First of all, we got to explain how you guys got older. So, what we have to do is move everybody up a rank. You become an admiral! And the rest of the cast become **Star Trek** commanders.'

And he tells me, 'One day, a force comes toward Earth — might be God, might be the devil— breaking everything in it's path, except the minds of the Star Ship commanders. So we gotta find all the original crewmen for the Starship *Enterprise*, but first where is Spock? He's back on Vulcan doing R&R; five-year mission — seven years of R&R. He swam back upstream. So we gotta go get him.' I call that show, *What Makes Salmon Run* ?

So we get Spock, do battle, and it was a great story!" And, of course, it led to a series of four more movies, the most recent of which was directed by Shatner himself.

SCIENCE
OFFICER

Report by Scott Nance

Spock wasn't the first Vulcan/human hybrid, according to Ambassador Sarek, his father. But he was the first to survive. "An Earth/Vulcan conception will abort during the end of the first month. The fetus is unable to continue life once it begins to develop its primary organs. The fetus Spock was removed from Amanda's body at this time, the first such experiment ever attempted.

"The tiny form resided in a test tube for the following two Earth months while our physicians performed delicate chemical engineering, including over a hundred subtle changes we hoped would sustain life. At the end of this time, the fetus was returned to Amanda's womb.

"At the end of the ninth Earth month, the tiny form was again removed from Amanda — prematurely by Vulcan standards—and spent the next four months of Vulcan-term pregnancy in a specially designed incubator. The infant Spock proved surprisingly resilient; seemed to be something about that Earth/Vulcan mixture which created in that tiny body the fierce determination to Survive," Ambassador Sarek once said (1).

Spock's first few years—when personality is largely determined—were confusing. On one side, he had Sarek, planting the seeds of Vulcan logic. On the other, the baby had the human Amanda acting as the natural, emotional, human mother. Although the custom in Sarek's family was to send young children off to "nannies" to begin their training in the Way, Amanda took full care of her son herself, every day, exposing her infant son to glaring emotions.

Sarek was concerned when Spock continued to display emotions. It was very embarrassing when he and his family visited other important Vulcans and his son would flagrantly laugh or raise his voice. Sarek could already see his son being shut out by other children his age. Spock's emotions frightened the others, and they began teasing him for it—a child's reaction to the different.

Spock's only real playmate was I'Chaya, the Sehlat that was once Sarek's. I'Chaya was like a huge brown teddy bear with six-inch fangs. The old beast was the most docile and playful creature alive. Spock would ride around the huge yard on his pet's back, having imaginary adventures in a fantasy world where he could be himself without worrying about the taunts of others.

With I'Chaya, Spock pretended he was a warrior leader of ancient Vulcan, leading his beast into war, fighting invisible enemies who rode invisible beasts. One day, he was charging into battle, and Sefek, a boy Spock's age, walked by. Spock, not seeing the visitor, fell off I'Chaya in pretend defeat. Sefek then unmercifully cut Spock down, calling him "weak" and "uncoordinated."

Sarek continued to tutor his son personally in the Vulcan disciplines. Spock had particular difficulty mastering the nerve-pinch. In his early days, he absorbed influences from both his parents, which seemed completely natural

PROFILE

since he did love and admire them both. Sarek's displeasure when Spock showed emotion confused the boy.

By about the age of six, Spock began to grasp the differences in his parents' systems of belief. He began to deeply understand the philosophy of logic, but at the same time, he couldn't let go of the emotions that his human mother imparted to him. Spock wanted to make both of his parents happy, but he wasn't happy. The other children still called him a "half-breed."

Upon his seventh year, Spock's father called on his son to make the most important decision of his life; to choose the Vulcan or the Human path. The human path seemed easier, with no controls on emotions. But he respected the Vulcan Way, and wanted to make his father proud. It *wouldn't* be easy.

Sarek was proud of his son's choice. It would've been easy for Spock to reject what was Vulcan, since much of Vulcan had rejected him. It had been Spock's emotions that caused the others to make fun of him, and it was those emotions that made the cruelty unbearable. They made the fantasy world he created with I'Chaya appealing.

Both Sarek and Amanda saw what their son was going through, and both felt his pain. Amanda was the one who expressed her sadness, coddling her son, "making it all better." Now Spock had finally chosen the Vulcan road, and the time for coddling was over. Sarek made that clear to both wife and child. Spock knew this, and agreed, wanting to be a real Vulcan.

Spock's decision was bittersweet for Amanda. Yes, she was proud of her son, but yet, she had half-hoped that he would've joined her road. She knew Sarek had been very permissive in letting her express her emotions towards Spock, but she also knew that emotions had to end. Earth would now be truly alien for Spock, and that saddened Amanda.

With Spock's decision came the kahs-wan, the test of manhood. He would have to exist alone in the desert to fully become a Vulcan. And Sarek added pressure on Spock to pass the kahs-wan on the first try to prove to all others that his son was worthy of his heritage.

That pressure ate away at Spock's untrained, underdeveloped emotions. If he failed, all would be lost, and he would always be "only a human."

Recently, a cousin of Sarek's family had joined the family for a visit on his way to a pilgrimage elsewhere. This cousin was Selek, and he soothed Spock. Selek seemed to understand young Spock very well.

One night, before the official test, Spock went out on his own kahs-wan to test himself. The sluggish old I'Chaya came with his young master. The cousin, Selek, also followed the boy, Spock, at a respectful distance. I'Chaya tried to defend his young master from an attacking le'matya, but the sehlet was too old to be very good at fighting. The le'matya poisoned I'Chaya. Selek moved in, and subdued the lizard, but it was too late for I'Chaya, who lay dying.

Selek stayed with the wounded beast while young Spock went to get a healer. When he returned it was already too late. The healer couldn't save I'Chaya. The healer could end I'Chaya's life quickly, painlessly, or I'Chaya could live on a little longer in agony. Spock had a decision to make. He took the course of ending the creature's pain.

Spock was a Vulcan, and his parents were proud. Selek, the cousin who had been so supportive and understanding of Spock, departed to continue his journey. No one in Sarek's family would see this mysterious figure again. This little test gave Spock the confidence he needed to pass the real kahs-wan.

With the manhood test behind him, and fully recognized as an official Vulcan, it was the appropriate time for the Vulcan bonding ritual. A mate would be arranged for Spock for later, when it came time for his ponn-farr. T'Pring, daughter of Saretek, a local dignitary on the Vulcan Council, was chosen as proper for Sarek's son.

Then Spock's real education began. He learned all Vulcan had to teach. It was rough going for Spock to keep his emotions in check. Amanda tried to conceal her own emotions, helping Spock manage his.

Although he excelled in all areas of academics, Spock particularly excelled in the sciences, where there was no place at all for emotion. This helped him to forget his own feelings. The Vulcan disciplines came harder than facts for Spock. They required a control of his emotions that was difficult. Any hint of emotion would block out his mind-melds and disrupt the concentration necessary for the nerve pinch.

Spock finally mastered the disciplines by the age of 12. He was still finding it hard to interact with his peers. Everyone remembered his outbursts of emotions from when he was younger. And no one forgot or forgave. Spock stayed on his own, continuing to learn, a pursuit he savored because he could do it alone.

Even as Spock achieved his adolescence, he remained alone, save for his parents and older tutors. Frustration built in Spock. Those early travails with the children crippled him socially later in life when he would stumble whenever he tried to reach out to others. This lack of "social graces" caused Spock great frustration.

Frustration led Spock to reject his people. Instead of trying, he turned inward, entering his own world of knowledge and fantasies. Spock dreamed of leaving Vulcan. He saw that as the only path to happiness. He wanted to leave Vulcan and use the scientific knowledge he was accumulating to prove to his people that he was worthy of being Vulcan.

Sarek remained proud of Spock over the years. He planned for his son to continue attending the Vulcan Science Academy, then finally becoming an instructor. Sarek was infuriated when his son instead announced he would be applying to Starfleet Academy for his higher education.

Sarek didn't want his son anywhere near that institution, which he saw as educationally inferior and run by human warmongers. Amanda was more supportive of her son. She felt it was his life, and that his course shouldn't be decided by Vulcan ritual. She believed Sarek and his family made a large enough mistake arranging a marriage for Spock.

Without even his father's support, alone, Spock packed his few things and went to the spaceport in Shi Kahr. He boarded the next ferry to Earth. At the Academy, his Vulcan heritage helped him to get into examination quickly. Starfleet was anxious to recruit Vulcans. Although it was easily the toughest examination of his life, Spock passed.

Spock found the psychological test especially difficult. In this test, he had to face his greatest fear. That wasn't easy for Starfleet to arrange. Spock had many internal fears, but he hid them all well. He was afraid of his father, other Vulcan children, but worst of all, Spock feared his own failure. He overcame this fear.

Spock was too distracted and distressed by his feud with his father to enjoy his new-found freedom. He remained introverted. Because Starfleet was eager to accommodate Spock, they gave him his own quarters which he could adjust to Vulcan norms. He didn't even have a roommate to socialize with.

Spock did meet a thin, blue Andorian who became his 3-D chess partner. But the Andorian dropped out after the first semester.

Spock enjoyed his classes, and continued to excel in the sciences. He soon took an interest in the theoretical sciences, which led to a paper published in the *Makropyrios Science Report*. This paper resulted in that prestigious university inviting Spock to take a semester of his training there. He accepted, and the Starfleet Academy was happy to oblige.

During his time at Makropyrios, Spock developed a friendship with Dr. Georges Mordreaux, a theoretical physicist and professor. Spock never enrolled in any of Dr. Mordreaux's classes, but he and Spock shared private discussions. Because of the continuing feud with his father, Mordreaux filled a paternal void.

At the end of the semester, Spock returned to Starfleet Academy to finish his education. After completing the initial training, he decided to go on to a year of Command School. Spock wasn't particularly interested in captaining a vessel, but felt he should prove himself to his father.

Command School involved practical work rather than the fact-gathering Spock preferred, but he did well, and this mandatory interpersonal work served to pull Spock "out of his shell." Spock's logical, unemotional reaction—almost a non-reaction—to the *Kobayashi Maru* no-win test scenario was in stark contrast to the shouting and screaming of his human peers. The human admiral conducting the test didn't know how to mark this first Vulcan. The admiral finally decided on "unique" as the most apt description.

After leaving Command School, Spock served his cadet cruise aboard the *USS Lexington* as an assistant science officer. Spock stood in awe of alien worlds which he visited. He had studied some of these worlds in school on Vulcan, but he now experienced them first-hand. Spock began to feel fulfilled. He still wasn't very happy and kept to himself. Many of the humans looked on him questioningly. Although Spock was half-human, it didn't physically show. To the humans, he remained an alien.

Spock officially distinguished himself on the *Lexington* as a top-rate science officer, working primarily in the fields of biology and chemistry. For his efforts to help end the Orion Beta Virus, Spock was awarded the Gold Star With Cluster.

At the end of his year-long cadet cruise, Spock earned the rank of full lieutenant, junior grade, skipping the rank of ensign entirely. He once again faced a decision. Starfleet, trying desperately to bring in more Vulcans, commissioned a heavy cruiser, the *USS Intrepid*, as the official Vulcan "flagship," to be manned exclusively by Vulcans. The Intrepid's first Vulcan crew of 430 ranked high in the Academy. Sumarek, the captain, had gained actual experience working for the Orion Merchant Marine.

In keeping with Vulcan's pacifist nature, the Intrepid would be strictly a science ship. They needed an experienced Vulcan to act as chief science officer. Command offered Spock the position, plus a promotion to lieutenant commander. But Spock didn't feel ready to return to the company of Vulcans. He wanted to be a complete success when he returned to Vulcan to prove wrong all those who doubted him. He declined the offer, and instead went aboard the human-run *Enterprise*.

The *Enterprise* had just finished its shakedown cruise with Captain Robert April at the helm. April, however, received a promotion to commodore and would be leaving the starship. Captain Christopher Pike gained the captaincy. Spock transferred to the relatively new ship as an assistant science officer. Pike and Spock took to each other easily. Both were reserved and distant from the crew. Both officers acted in measured steps, although they both felt deep and powerful emotions they kept under tight control.

After a year in space, the chief science officer departed for a teaching position at the Academy. Pike immediately promoted Spock. Besides their ease working together, Spock had proved himself efficient and dedicated. Spock constantly tried to prove himself to Captain Pike, considering the Captain his first real friend.

The years passed at warp speed. The crew finished one five year mission, and within six months embarked on a second. Starfleet knew deep space was unfolding too quickly to slow the pace. Starfleet pushed everyone to the edge of known space and into the unknown to reap benefits from the expensive dozen heavy cruisers it had built.

Spock was assigned to head the science department. Although still a touch reticent, he worked well with the rest of the crew. They were all quite friendly. The first officer, known only as "Number One," shared the Vulcan trait for non-emotion, and thereby shared an unspoken empathy with the Vulcan science officer.

For yet another five years, Spock continued to win awards and commendations, inside and out of Starfleet. He used his Command School training to lead science teams away from the ship on first encounters with alien planets. Spock won special commendations for his close work with the command crew in the Talos IV incident, which closed the world to outsiders.

After this second five-year mission, Captain Pike was transferred to Starfleet Command as fleet captain. Following another six-month overhaul, the *Enterprise* set out again. The crew was almost completely different. The new command crew—the captain, first officer and chief engineer—were all very emotional, outgoing individuals. First Officer Gary Mitchell wasn't above telling Vulcan jokes within earshot of Spock. Spock, now a lieutenant commander, didn't know how his relationship would turn out with his new captain, James Tiberius Kirk.

(1) Interview with Gene Roddenberry on "Inside Star Trek" (Columbia Records, 1976)

"I had started out with a love of the theatre," Nimoy states, "but came to California to pursue a film career. I always felt that I would work here until I developed enough of a reputation to be useful on the road and on Broadway."

Leonard Nimoy made his initial foray into movies in the theatrical version of **Queen for a Day** in 1951. He appears as a supporting character in the "High Diver" segment of this anthology film. This was followed by **Rhubarb** in which he plays one of the members of a baseball team inherited by a cat.

His first starring role came in his third feature film appearance when he was cast in the lead of the 1952 film **Kid Monk Baroni**, a boxing picture about a youth (Nimoy), who has a deformed face and becomes a successful fighter until he has plastic surgery. It's a film with strange morals as a priest convinces Baroni to go back into the ring after his facial surgery so that he can win money for the church!

Nimoy returned to the ranks of supporting players in **Francis Goes to West Point, Zombies of the Stratosphere** and the Republic B-western **Old Overland Trail** in which he has a small role as an Indian chief named Black Hawk. In the science fiction monster classic **Them!** (1954) his role is even smaller as he has a walk-on part as a soldier delivering a message which has just come over the radio.

In 1954, Nimoy met a young actress named Sandi Zober and married her. Their first 18 months of marriage were spent in Georgia while Nimoy served out his stint in the U.S. Army. Stationed at Fort McPhearson, he was in Special Services—writing, narrating and emceeing GI shows. In his spare time he worked with the Atlanta Theatre Guild where he directed and played the role of Stanley in "A Streetcar Named Desire."

Upon his discharge from the Army, Nimoy resumed his acting career in Hollywood. He worked with Jeff Corey, first as a student, then as an instructor in Corey's classes. Next, Nimoy operated his own drama studio in North Hollywood for three years and taught for a year at Synanon.

By this time Nimoy's two children had been born and he had to supplement his modest income from teaching and acting. Such jobs included driving a cab, working in a pet shop and as an usher in a movie house.

Nimoy's career started moving again in the early Sixties when bit parts on TV shows grew into meatier roles on such shows as **Rawhide, The Virginian, Outer Limits** and **Profiles in Courage**. As evidenced by the episodic TV listing elsewhere in this volume, his credits cover most of the top shows on the air at the time. Because of his rugged features, he was usually cast as the heavy in his early roles. His first sympathetic role in years was in a **Dr. Kildare** directed by his past mentor, Elliot Silverstein. Speaking of the actor, award-winning director Silverstein states, "Nimoy is one of the most patient actors I've met. He's remained gentle and dignified throughout, even when he wasn't welcome as a first-line talent as he is today. He has a gentleness and sweetness of disposition that always seeps through. He's probably one of the best trained actors around, with a steadiness of purpose which results in his be-

THE ACTOR

ing able to bear the various degrees of recognition heaped on actors through their careers. He's grown as a man and therefore as an actor, rather than the reverse."

On stage, Nimoy appeared as Izquierdo in "Monserrat" and Brick in "Cat On A Hot Tin Roof." During his 1968 hiatus from **Star Trek** he starred in Gore Vidal's comedy, "Visit to a Small Planet" at the Pheasant Run Playhouse in Chicago. His role as an alien who visits Earth must had had particular impact then since he was simultaneously appearing on TV as Mr. Spock.

During the summer of 1971 he starred in "Fiddler on the Roof" appearing at the Town and Country Playhouse in Rochester, Ohio's Masonic Auditorium and at the North Shore Music Theatre and Cape Cod Melody Tent, both in Massachusetts.

Nimoy entered the recording field early in 1967 on the Dot Label. His first album, "Leonard Nimoy Presents Mr. Spock's Music From Outer Space," enjoyed a sale of 130,000 copies and produced a hot single, "Visit To A Sad Planet." It was followed by four more Dot albums. In the Seventies he made five narrative albums for Caedmon records, including readings from H.G. Wells' *War of the Worlds* and Ray Bradbury's *The Martian Chronicles*.

In 1971, Nimoy had third billing under Yul Brynner and Richard Crenna in **Catlow**. Just as Shatner has his nude scene in **Big Bad Mama**, Nimoy's came in the Western, **Catlow**.

In the **Mission: Impossible**-style TV movie **The Alpha Caper** (1974), Nimoy played opposite Henry Fonda. Only unlike that earlier series, this was a gang of thieves who pulled off a crime like clockwork only to be tripped up by fate.

The less said about the TV movie **The Missing Are Deadly** (1975) the better. Although he has second billing, Nimoy's role has everything from A to B.

Although the 1978 remake of **Invasion of the Body Snatchers** garnered mixed reviews and mediocre boxoffice returns, Nimoy's role was singled out as being some of his best work in years.

In 1975, at age 44, Nimoy entered college while continuing to carry out dozens of acting assignments, and won a master;s degree in education from Antioch College.

In 1977, Nimoy received positive critical notices as Martin Dysart in the play "Equus."

From 1978 through 1981, Nimoy toured the country in the one-man play, "Vincent." It was written and directed by Nimoy, based on the play "Van Gogh" by Phillip Stephens. Nimoy gave over 150 performances during this time and it was videotaped and broadcast on the Arts & Entertainment cable channel.

In 1978, Nimoy settled a long-outstanding grievance with Paramount Pictures when he signed for **Star Trek: The Motion Picture** and reportedly received $3.5 million, which included payment in compensation for the use of his likeness during the years of merchandizing Mr. Spock.

Aside from acting and directing, Nimoy's favorite creative outlet is photography and writing. He specializes in black and white studies. Some of his work has appeared in public shows. He has also written a handful of books including **I Am Not Spock** as well as several volumes of poetry beginning with **Why Not You and I?** which is illustrated with his own photographs.

In 1986 Nimoy separated from his wife of 32 years and several months later divorce proceedings began.

Nimoy's first two stints as director on a feature film were for **Star Trek III** and **IV. Three Men and a Baby**, released in 1987, is his third and has grossed over $100 million. Work on his fourth directing stint, **The Good Mother** was held up by his participation in **Star Trek V**. Finally released in late '88, **The Good Mother** garnered mixed reviews and poor boxoffice returns.

Although the revival of Star Trek gave Nimoy additional career opportunities, he has demonstrated that there can be life after Star Trek. Whether this will interfere with future sequels remains to be seen. What doesn't have to remain to be seen is that, now in his late Fifties, Nimoy's career shows no signs of slowing down.

With the release of **Star Trek IV**, Leonard Nimoy had became even more deeply involved with **Star Trek** than he'd even been during the initial run of 79 episodes. It didn't start out that way, though, as he was just one of the cast on **Star Trek: The Motion Picture.** He was in a position to learn from everyone else's mistakes. That film had not been a particularly pleasant experience for Nimoy, and it led directly to his desire to have Spock killed off in **Star Trek II.** From his standpoint now as director of the third and fourth features, he can look at them from a larger perspective.

"In deference to the people who made the first **Star Trek** motion picture, they had a very special set of problems to deal with," Nimoy begins. "For example, there had not been a **Star Trek** project for eleven years. They finished the series in '68 and here we were in 1979 coming together again to do a new **Star Trek**. That meant that a lot of special circumstances had to be addressed. The ice had to be broken in a special kind of way. Do you comment in the film about the fact that the crew has not been together in eleven years? Do you act as if eleven years have passed and things have changed? The ship has changed. Uniforms have changed. Sets have changed. Rank has changed. Relationships have changed. We were faced with the concern that we should not be perceived as a blown-up television episode—that we should be looked upon as a motion picture. Therefore it was believed that certain changes were expected by the audience and must be addressed."

Also complicating the making of the film was that they were coming in on the heels of **Star Wars**, which had created an entirely new set of audience expectations and a whole new climate for science fiction films.

"By the way, we were grateful to **Star Wars** for having established that climate," Nimoy is quick to add. "I'm convinced that it's the success of **Star Wars** in 1977 that caused somebody over at Paramount to say, 'Hey, we've got one of those called **Star Trek**. Let's do it.' So that got us off the ground. But that **Star Wars** atmosphere had to be dealt with because it was an atmosphere of a very physical, special effect, large-looking motion picture as compared to what **Star Trek** episodes offered, which was, a lot of times, actors interacting with each other."

Thus the film played up special effects and downplayed the characters.

"In **Star Trek: The Motion Picture** we spent a lot of time staring at a view screen on which a lot of special effects would be added later. So the climate was problematic.

"Personally, **Star Trek I** was not my favorite," Nimoy admits. "I think it was very tastefully produced and presented, and obviously a very well-crafted film. And certainly Paramount showed that they were serious about making as fine a picture as possible. They bit the bullet financially. We started out with a 15 million dollar budget and they let it expand to 45 million dollars on that movie."

The director feels that the elements which made a story real **Star Trek** really came together much better on the second film.

INTERVIEW

"I think Harv (Bennett) and the people that he gathered around him put the series back on track with **Star Trek II**. He put us back in touch with the characters, and put us back in touch with some of the humor, the energy, the attitude and the colorful aspects, if you will, of **Star Trek** the series."

Which brings us up to **The Search for Spock**, the first of the two films in the series which Nimoy directed.

"I came on trying to make the third better than the second. How do you do that? Well, I would be the first to say that stepping in as director on **Star Trek III** and directing for the first time on **Star Trek**, I still had a tremendous benefit, which is my knowledge of the history of **Star Trek** and the elements that I believed made **Star Trek** cook that I believed had not been totally tapped as yet, even in **Star Trek II**. So I had the advantage of knowing where there were secret pockets lying around that they had not gotten in touch with yet."

After the third film was finished, Nimoy and Bennett were asked by Paramount to develop a concept for **Star Trek IV**.

"We had not yet done a time travel story in the movies and time travel had been used very successfully in the series. I felt very strongly, and Harv agreed, that in the films they had been doing the black hat bad guys where it was us against him. I felt very strongly that we should not do that again, and that doing that a third time in a row would be a mistake, that it would not be good **Star Trek** to continue to play against a bad guy. Some of our best episodes had no bad guy. We had circumstances. We had problems, and we had conditions that we had to deal with and I felt that we should do that now in the new film.

"In a way, by making that decision, we were already setting up a frame of fresh territory for ourselves and avoiding a trap which would have produced a very linear series of films in that it would be very difficult to prove that each was better than the last because they would be compared, apples to apples to apples. Do they get bigger and shinier or don't they? In doing what I just described, setting up a new premise in which the adversary was circumstances rather than the individual, we were now becoming an orange instead of an apple, so it would be fresh territory for us."

Arriving at the idea to do a time travel movie meant arriving at the decision as to which era to visit. It seemed obvious to the film-makers that going with a contemporary setting offered more possibilities as had been so ably demonstrated by the episodes "Tomorrow Is Yesterday" and 'Assignment Earth."

"It seemed more fun cinematically to be among us, on the streets of San Francisco today, than to go to other times," Nimoy explains, although he also adds that, "We explored all sorts of time possibilities. We went all the way back to prehistoric times and even one or two hundred years into the future. But it just made sense to us that it was going to be a lot of fun to have these archetypes from **Star Trek** on the streets of San Francisco today.

"In discussions about why we were traveling back in time, you come up with various possibilities. Maybe you are transported accidentally. For example, we are on a strange ship. We are not that familiar with its cloaking device. We could kick in the cloaking device to escape an enemy and find that we've made a mistake and it kicks us in with time travel accidentally. Or, we could be chasing somebody, as we did in 'City On The Edge Of Forever.' These possibilities were all discussed."

Once the time travel angle had been established, there had to be a reason for the voyage, and this also had to be arrived at.

"We talked at great length about the various possibilities based upon the concept that there was a problem in the 24th century and that what was needed to solve that problem had been lost and could only be found in the 20th century. That could be a person who had a skill that is gone in the 24th century. We talked about the fact that by the 24th century we will probably not crack oil on this planet, oil having been depleted to the point where we have to replace it as an energy source, and if we had to crack oil in the 24th century we probably would have to come back and find a guy with a hard-hat in Texas and take him to the future to help us out.

"Then we talked about the possibility of diseases that might be taking place in the future, the cure for which might be in a plant which exists today but will be gone 50 to 100 years from now. But the idea of carrying a plant through 300 years of time in a spaceship didn't look extremely cinematic and I was also not really excited about the idea of seeing gobs and gobs of sick people lying around dying on screen in what was hopefully going to be a piece of entertainment.

"And then one night, sitting around with a friend of mine, talking about endangered species, we came up with the subject of the humpback whale and it seemed to offer a lot that we were looking for. It had the size, the mystery and the majesty of these gigantic creatures. And it had the sounds they make, and we really don't know what that sound is for."

At one point, there were discussions about translating the sound of the whales, and of the probe, on the screen.

"We went around and around about that right down to the final weeks of editing the film. There was some discussion as to whether or not we should put subtitles on the screen. But it was felt by some that it might be off-putting to an audience. Or else some people might feel like they were missing something and ask, 'Well, what are they saying to each other?' I resisted it for my reasons and others wanted it for their reasons. I felt, finally, that to leave it a mystery is much more dramatic, exciting and profound than trying to explain it literally."

By this time, Nimoy felt that he had gone through a testing process on the first three films. He felt freer to be more explosive in ideas and more dynamic in presentation, "To be a little bit more demanding of myself, and hopefully that's on the screen."

Nimoy felt freer to indulge in the use of humor, which had largely been forbidden in the first film and cites the following example.

"At the very end of **Star Trek: The Motion Picture**, when the adventure was over and we were on the bridge shooting the final good-bye scene, and Kirk is addressing the various characters who have gathered for this mission and is offering to return them to the place he'd picked them up. McCoy, who'd just come out of retirement, said something to the effect of, 'Well, I'm here, I might as well stay.' Then he turned to Spock and said he'll be back on Vulcan shortly, and as it was written, Spock was to say, 'My work on Vulcan is finished.' In the final rehearsal, when McCoy said, 'I'm here, I might as well stay,' I said, 'If Doctor McCoy is to remain on board, my presence here will be essential.' You won't see that in the movie—it was not allowed. There was a very fast conference of all the grey heads and they said that it didn't seem appropriate because people have died and it's a very serious movie....

"We've come a long way since then and have learned the value of laughter. It was one of the wonderful ingredients of the series and a great source of energy. So, in general, that was the approach we took with the fourth film."

Although it was rumored that additional footage had been shot with George Takei and the helicopter, Nimoy states that this isn't so. "What we shot is what you saw. All we wanted to do is establish that he's there and has a helicopter."

Nimoy does reveal that there was some other footage which was shot and not used involving the Christine Chapel character.

"There was one piece of footage of Chapel, maybe the only piece of film in the movie that didn't survive. It's a small scene of her outside the council chamber as Sarek was arriving for the first scene. We see him arrive, see her greet him, and he says something like, 'How is it going?' and she replies, 'Not well,' and they go inside. In the editing it seemed best to go right to the excitement of that stuff on the screen and have Sarek come out of the shadows as his entrance rather than be introduced outside. There was also other footage of Chapel and Janice Rand reporting for command during the disaster periods of the rain sequence and so forth which weren't needed."

In spite of being as close to the film as he is, Nimoy is still able to be objective about his work on **Star Trek IV**.

"Here and there are things I might have attacked differently, but I'm pretty pleased with this movie. There are moments when I sit and wonder, 'Am I getting away with this or am I not?' I know what's going on here, but does the audience? I'm always worried about the computer room scene when Spock leaves the bridge and says, 'I'm going to the computer room to see if my theory is correct,' and McCoy and Kirk follow and we open on that monitor of the computer putting together an image with the information and the sound. We played that entire scene in one take with no coverage and one might say, gee, you should have punched in a little bit here and there and given up moments where Kirk is trying to figure it out and Spock is giving him answers and McCoy is casting doubt. My personal relief comes at the end of the scene when Kirk starts to get the idea and McCoy starts to get the idea that Kirk is getting the idea at the same time and says, 'Now wait just a damn minute,' and the audience responds and I go, 'Oh, they got it!' So there are moments like that which are scary. But on the other hand, I was trying to make this film more of a visual spectacle because we had the money to do it."

Nimoy has since directed two other films, **Three Men and a Baby** and **The Good Mother**. On **Star Trek V**, Nimoy stood back once more while another director took over. A newcomer by the name of William Shatner. Whether Nimoy will be tapped to direct **Star Trek** again in the future remains to be seen.

THE
DOCTOR

Growing up in the southeastern region of the Pan-Terra Union— Old Earth's Deep South of the United States of America —had a profound effect on Leonard McCoy. Four hundred years after the American Civil War, the South retained a culture and pride that found its way into many facets of Leonard's personality. Even as a young child, Leonard was a calm, relaxed sort. Just as the other natives he enjoyed long evening strolls under the magnolia trees; but he could become passionate and fiery when something disturbed his sense of what was right.

Leonard was born to Harrison and Caroline McCoy. Harrison — Harry — was a Starfleet engineer aboard the then-new starship, the *USS Yorktown*. Caroline worked for her father-in-law, T.J. McCoy, as his medical assistant. Several years before, she had met Harry through her job, and this was where she went back to work after Harry disappeared in deep space aboard the Yorktown.

Len's grandfather T.J. would have described himself as "just an ol' country doctor." T.J. was a physician who refused to rely solely on gadgets but instead depended on stubbornness and faith in the healing powers of the human body. After school and on weekends, young Leonard would visit his grandfather's office and watch T.J. search through a time-worn book for answers the medical diagnostics computer couldn't give.

T.J. and Len were shocked and grief-stricken when Caroline was killed in a hovercraft accident while visiting her parents on Deneb IV. Death touched Len closely for the first time, and he hated it. T.J. tried to comfort his grandson as much as he could. Leonard felt very alone in the world, and T.J. tried hard to fill that void. T.J. took Leonard on many weekend camping and fishing trips in the wilderness preserves near Atlanta.

"When me and my grandaddy were off camping together, I felt like the whole universe wasn't any bigger than the two of us," wrote Len in his journal. "I was secure in a world that I knew about, and I felt like somebody gave a damn. In Atlanta everything was huge and empty, as if no one knew about me, and no one wanted to know. When I wasn't doing something with my grandad, I was usually holed up with one of his old-fashioned medical books, daydreaming about being an ol' country doctor."

One of the few bright spots in Len's high school years was his relationship with Nancy. "Nancy was really sweet. I wasn't the most outgoing guy around, but she went out of her way to talk to me, to get to know me. I guess I was a little surprised that a girl would like me that much. She used to call me 'plum'. Looking back, I think I mistook that overwhelming surprise and Nancy's fondness for me for love. I was sure we were in love with each other. It went on this way for a long while. I paraded around with her, and I thought, 'Boy, this is great. We're in love and we're going to ride off and spend our lives together.

"Things just didn't work out that way. She met an older man. A doctor of something or other, named Crater. Right as I was going to propose, Nancy told me that our relationship together shouldn't be 'quite so involved, Plum dear',

PROFILE

that she wanted the space to get to know Crater. Once that happened, I just had this feeling in the pit of my stomach that I'd lost out. I kept thinking, 'This is just silly, she's trying to let me down easy. It has to end.' And I'll be damned if it didn't do just that. Nancy told me she had fallen in love with Crater and that he had proposed, that she had accepted, and they were moving to a distant planet so he could continue his 'revolutionary research.' Ah, to be pretty much alone...."

Without Nancy, Len focused himself more clearly and devoted his life to going to medical school the year after he graduated from high school. Academics had gone well for Len. He was in the top quarter of his class, and T.J. had already recommended his grandson for his own alma mater: Emory University Medical Training Center.

However, a month before Len matriculated, his grandfather, T.J., was rushed to Atlanta's medical center after a massive heart attack. T.J. died a few hours later. Two days later, Len made the funeral arrangements. When Len came home from the funeral, he poured himself a good shot of Jack Daniel's finest in his grandfather's memory. "My grandaddy was gone, and I was truly alone. He had been my best friend since I could remember. He believed in me even when I didn't. T.J. McCoy had been a damn extraordinary man, and I want to keep his memory alive through what I do," wrote Len.

Len McCoy spent most of his medical training in quiet solitude. He studied with a drink in hand, and his work and his drink would put him to sleep most nights. The only enjoyment Len got out of life was his medical work, especially the hands-on observation of the physicians he trained under. The book work went easily for Len because having read his grandfather's books all his life, the classroom was mostly review. It was the actual interaction with patients that put a glow in Len. To see a patient come in ill or injured, perhaps frightened, and to help this living being heal, both bodily and emotionally, to see this patient fully recovered, reunited with his loved ones, and a smile on his face was what Len lived for.

Len appreciated a comprehensive approach to healing, the kind his grandfather practiced. He believed in the body, in its own abilities to heal. Len saw himself more as a teacher rather than a mechanic. He believed in the mind and body as one, and knew that a patient couldn't get well unless he was ready mentally and emotionally. Len wanted to escape gadgetry and concentrate on helping people gain confidence in their own healing properties.

Although he continued to drink, Len did well. He was still haunted by his loneliness. "One night I can recall particularly," wrote Len. "The ward was all quiet and empty except for one old woman whose cancer had gone through her whole body. When she was conscious, she was in a lot of pain. But right then she was sleeping peacefully, and I was watching over her.

"We had become close during her several months in the ward. She had been an ol' Southern belle; she had known my family for years. She used to visit my grandad's dad, and she told great yarns, those really good ol' Southern stories. Anyway, that night she had fallen asleep and I spent — had to be eight hours just sitting at her bedside in this eerie faint light. By morning she was dead. It was the first time I had ever seen anyone die, but she died at peace.

"People have said, 'Leonard McCoy hates death,' and other malarkey like that. Hating death is nonsense; its part of the universe. When people are ready to die, they die; I just don't want people dying before their time. That's what I've spent my life for, making sure people don't die before whatever cosmic scheme you believe in tells them to die. Maybe what I believe is horse hockey, I don't know, but that's my great philosophy on life and death."

That old woman's death showed Len that no matter what, you're alone in the world. That's how he felt. Toward the end of his medical training, Len was lifted by two events: one was the Atlanta General Hospital offering him a residency, the other was meeting a woman named Honey.

The occurrence of the two were practically simultaneous. Len met Honey Longfield when he went to the hospital for his interview. Honey was there as a patient waiting to see the same doctor Len had to see about a job. This doctor's previous meeting ran late, so Len and Honey began chatting, and getting to know each other. He charmed Honey Southern-style with gallant notions of saving lives. Honey was also attracted to Len's old-fashioned romantic nature.

Honey and Len began dating, and after three months, Len proposed. Two months later, they were married. Subconsciously, if not consciously, Len didn't want Honey to get away like Nancy did. Len was alone, and he desperately grabbed hold of any chance not to be alone anymore. He wanted a special person to share his life with. Soon after their marriage, Len began his job at the hospital and he and his wife set up a home in Atlanta.

Money wasn't abundant in the new McCoy household. This lack soon became a sore spot in the marriage. Len's residency wasn't lucrative. The McCoys lived comfortably, and when their daughter Joanna arrived, she was well cared-for, but this new family wasn't living up to the wealthy Southern "quality folk" standard that Honey had in mind. She kept pushing her husband into a higher-paying private practice, but Len wanted to work in a hospital where he felt he could make more of a difference in emergency life or death matters.

Honey also resented the twelve, fourteen, sometimes twenty-four hours shifts Len put in at the hospital. She told him he was neglecting his family. As the tension rose, Len stayed away more and more just to keep out of Honey's tirades. Len began heavily drinking once again. "With me, the patients came first. They were the ones down and out. They were the ones who needed my real skills. I never wanted to hurt my family. Especially Joanna. She was always a real cute kid. After being alone for so long it was wonderful how this little person needed me so much," Len wrote.

One hot Summer night after coming home from a long shift at the hospital, Len dragged himself to the bar and poured a stiff drink to shield himself from the tantrum from Honey he knew was coming, but she had gone. And had taken Joanna. For weeks, he tried to track down his family, but to no avail. Honey finally reappeared in the form of a divorce notice and a custody notice. Len tried to fight the custody decision, but was unsuccessful when the issue of his drinking was raised.

After his family was broken asunder, Len continued to work long shifts at the hospital, until the funding for his residency was taken away during sweeping funding cuts. The United Federation of Planets and its members were reallocating money away from other services and directing them toward Starfleet in order to combat Klingon expansion near the Federation border.

Unemployed, Len read a recruiting ad for Starfleet. As he later said, "It was the only game in town." Doctors were in high demand in Starfleet, so Len was allowed a short orientation in lieu of Starfleet Academy. Len was commissioned in as a lieutenant, and assigned to a starbase near to the action. Starfleet was battling Klingon privateers masquerading as pirates along a disputed strategic zone.

Casualties were running high, and Len fought the kind of needless death he hated with a passion. Combat weary scouts, destroyers, and frigates came to the starbase for repair and medical treatment for their crews; Len saw injured and tired officers all day and all night. Many died. It was three in the morning planetside and Len was tired and aching when the emergency technicians carried in an officer with burns and contusions. The man was conscious, and as per procedure filled out his own treatment sheet. As Len looked it over he was shocked to find that this man was Harry McCoy.

After the rescue of the Yorktown years before, Harry was never recovered. The Yorktown had been hunting Orion pirates, and Harry had been one of a group of officers the Orions captured after they boarded the starship. Harry had finally been freed in a prisoner swap between the Orion government and the UFP, but he was unable to locate his family on Earth after T.J. and Caroline's deaths.

"To say I was shocked would be a damned understatement," wrote Len. "We had all written my dad off for dead years ago. I'd call our meeting a miracle."

Harry recovered quickly on the starbase, while father and son caught up on each other's lives. Harry and his son would go drinking together in the starbase officer's lounge, playing long games of 3-D chess. After Harry was well, he returned to duty aboard a short-range scout ship. He returned to the starbase occasionally, and Len was more than eager to become close to his father.

Several years went by on the starbase, days slipping one into the next, Len trying to regain lost years each time his father came to the planet. Each time an emptiness slipped between the two, an emptiness that spanned the years of their separation.

One afternoon, Harry's ship limped into starbase. Len learned Orion pirates had ambushed the ship. After a hard battle, the Starfleet vessel had escaped, but not unscathed. The phaser couplings had exploded while Harry McCoy was watching over them. Harry was doused in a huge radiation bath, inducing a crippling disease. Harry was remanded to starbase due to poor health.

Len did everything for his father, supporting him emotionally. Yet Len was continually failing in his desperate attempt to find a cure to his father's eventually-fatal illness. The contrast between his outward show of happiness and his inward frustration and self-doubt was killing Len as fast as the radiation was killing his father. Finally Harry slipped into an irrevocable coma. He lay in sickbay in stasis for months while Len prayed he would recover. After a night of drinking memorials to his father, in the sobering light of morning, Len ordered the med techs to disconnect his father's stasis, and Harry McCoy slipped into quiet death. No disappearances, no turning up in his son's arms miraculously again. This time it was truly over.

Months later Len was reading a medical journal when he stumbled across a successful antidote for his father's affliction that had been developed on Altair VI.

"I wanted off that blasted starbase. I kept expecting my daddy to walk off one of those ships that docked every day. I had been given my second chance to know my father, and I screwed it up. I always pushed so hard to be my daddy's best ol' son, but I didn't even feel like he was a real father. And I don't think he thought I was his real son, either," Len wrote.

With the Klingon expansion that first brought Len into the service over, it was easy to get a transfer to the USS Enterprise with a promotion to lieutenant commander and chief medical officer. The CMO on the Enterprise, Dr. Paul Piper, was leaving because of "personality conflicts" with the ship's new captain, James Kirk. Piper called Kirk "too unorthodox," and Len thought a dose of good ol' fashioned unorthodoxy was just what the doctor ordered. His life began anew aboard the Starship Enterprise.

Before Dr. McCoy came numerous television, stage and screen roles as villains for DeForest Kelley. The role of Dr. Leonard "Bones" McCoy changed Kelley's life. As McCoy he portrays an outspoken realist with an acid wit, a highly practical "general practitioner."

DeForest was born in Atlanta, Georgia in 1920, where he graduated from high school sixteen years later. At seventeen he made his first trip outside the state, visiting an uncle in Long Beach, California. He went for two weeks but stayed for a year. Upon returning home, Kelley told his mother, "I have a terrible shock for you. I am going to go and live in California."

This decision did not set well with his parents. His infatuation with the entertainment world was foreign to his father, a Southern Baptist minister. But his mother encouraged rather than discouraged his artistic talents. She realized the limitations of Atlanta for the son of a Baptist minister and had earlier cleared the way for him to sing in the church choir. For a time he'd done solo work and eventually sang on a program on radio station WSB. For this he won an engagement at the Atlanta Paramount Theatre singing with Lew Forbes and his orchestra.

Long Beach changed his entire future. Joining the Long Beach Theatre Group, he formed a radio group with his friend Barney Girard. Barney wrote the plays and the rest of the group put them on at the local radio station. Off the air, Kelley earned his living as an elevator operator.

During the war, Kelley was spotted in a Navy training film by a Paramount scout. This resulted in a screen test and a contract. He remained with the studio for two and one-half years.

In 1948, Kelley went east to New York, gaining experience in stock, stage and television. Upon returning to California he discovered that Hollywood has a short memory. Many of the people he had known in New York were now working on the West Coast, such as his friend Barney Girard, who was writing for the **You Are There** TV series. They helped De Forest re-establish himself in the film capital.

Numerous TV appearances followed, including roles on **Schlitz Theatre, Playhouse 90, Gunsmoke, You Are There, Navy Log, Science Fiction Theatre, Zane Grey Theatre, Rawhide** and **Bonanza.**

He also took parts in motion pictures, including for such films as **Fear in the Night** (in which he had a leading role), **Canon City, Gunfight at Comanche Creek, Illegal, Marriage on the Rocks** and **The Men.** Other films included **Variety Girl, View from Pompey's Head, Waco** and **Duke of Chicago. House of Bamboo, Tension at Table Rock, Gunfight at the O.K. Corral, Raintree County, The Law and Jake Wade, Black Spurs, Town Tamer, Warlock, Gunfight, Johnny Reno, Apache Uprising, Where Love Has Gone,** and **Night of the Lepus** provided other parts for Kelley. He was becoming known for playing character parts, particularly in Westerns.

THE ACTOR

"For ten years I played Western heavies mainly," said Kelley. "Then Gene Roddenberry considered me for a part and asked if I had any objections to doing my hair differently. I had been wearing it long, for westerns."

Roddenberry wanted a brainy, Kennedy look and asked Kelley to go to Jay Sebring, a famous men's hair stylist in Hollywood.

"It was expensive," said Kelley. "It cost me thirty-five dollars, but I had confidence in Roddenberry. The part was that of a lawyer in a TV pilot, that remained unsold. Then Roddenberry cast Kelley as McCoy.

"I'd never been in a series before," he explained. "I made a drastic change with this role. Roddenberry went out on a limb for me. The town had forgotten the actor I used to be. Then Roddenberry pulled me out of a big rut. I feel very lucky."

Often a casting call for a role in a network television series attracts dozens of hopeful applicants. The **Star Trek** television series cast no less than three different actors in the role of ship's doctor.

"You know that John Hoyt played the first doctor," recounts DeForest Kelley, the actor who played Doctor Leonard "Bones" McCoy, **Star Trek**'s most famous physician. "And then Paul Fix did it in the second pilot. Paul Fix was a wonderful character actor who had done a lot of Westerns. Hoyt, of course, was a different kind of personality, a very elegant man and a marvelous actor.

"The way the role came about for me is that I had done a pilot film for Gene Roddenberry in 1960 called **333 Montgomery**, where I portrayed a criminal lawyer in San Francisco named Jake Erlich. Edmund O'Brien finally did it. But Roddenberry wrote a beautiful script and we shot the whole thing in San Francisco and I was really chosen for the role by Erlich. He looked at all the tests that were made for him, and that was my first experience with Gene. And then I did . . . he wanted me for this show, but I had been doing nothing but villains and the network didn't think that would go well with a country doctor type of guy, I suppose. So he failed. I went ahead and did another pilot for Gene called **Police Story**. As you know, Gene was a cop for eight years, and it was another good show that was more or less ahead of its time. But they sent the show out on these reaction showings where they press these little buttons if they like you or dislike you, so, somehow or another I got a rather high rating on that. I had called Gene to thank him for giving me the shot in the pilot (which didn't sell), and he said, 'Don't hang up, NBC has changed their mind and have decided to go with you as the doctor on **Star Trek**. So I started on the first episode, but I was not in either one of the two pilots."

"Gene screened that for me when they were going to do the series," Kelley recalls, "and that's where I saw Hoyt do the part, and even though it was a very small scene that he did, I was very taken with it. I was very impressed by his relationship with the captain, and I felt that the part had a chance to grow and become an interesting role."

Kelley explains that prior to the fourth **Star Trek** film he had done very little comedy. "I went out several years ago in a play, just to do an out-and-out comedy, called **Beginner's Luck**, a show that Bob Crane was doing around the country. It was strictly a farce type of thing, and I had a great time doing it, but I was trying to do something that was entirely different than I had been doing. The only other comedy to amount to anything that I did was in **Star Trek** in the series."

At some point in time, every actor or actress in every television series is asked to explain the enduring and endearing qualities of their show. This is especially true for the cast of **Star Trek**, a series with millions of fans in all walks of life. Kelley takes his turn, "There's so many things that it makes you wonder. You got one idea one time and then you turn around and, sure enough, that can't be it. I don't know, the thing seems to have touched a chord with people from all walks of life. It's all mystifying in a way. In the beginning, when it started in '66, it was really the first multi-racial cast that came about in televi-

INTERVIEW

sion. It was an optimistic show, to say the least, and it presented a new and bright future. It showed the young people of this country that there is some place to go and they haven't got there really yet, and that's in space, and it's the greatest ocean in the world. I think they enjoyed the comradeship among the cast, that these people showed unabashed love and affection for each other and they were a bunch of experts moving around in a bizarre world doing a good job. And somewhere along the line we always tried to lay in some message very subtly that might be appealing."

Convention audiences "can philosophize on the show to such a depth that they go beyond me or my way of thinking," Kelley continues. "To avoid those kinds of questions, I usually say, 'I'm a doctor, not a philosopher. They're curious about the people that worked on the show; they're curious about the directors; and they're curious about the stories we do. They sometimes question why we did certain things in there; I can't field them all. They go beyond us sometimes.

"You must remember that they have seen us for so many years on the screen and that a great part of the whole thing is for them to be able to meet you and ask you a question personally. That has a great deal to do with it , because so many of them never get a chance to come here or to see us and it's just the personal contact. For a long time I did autograph sessions afterward. But that got completely out of hand, because the crowds were too big; you can't accommodate them all.

"They have been a very devoted audience with us, and as a matter of fact, the only reason we were on the air in the third year was because of that audience. The letters that they wrote to the network put us on the air for the third year or they would have dropped us after the second year. And they've been with us all the way through this (the movies), too. And not only are they with us, but now their children and some of the children's children."

"I think that there's a great deal more that we could do (with my character). We fought to get **Star Trek** back to somewhere where it was from the first motion picture. But it's been very difficult to flesh out the characters or to have a chance to let the characters grow, because you throw out one movie, you know, and you've got to try to satisfy a lot of people with one. If we were doing a series, we could do some interesting things with the characters as they move along. That's the only reason that I approached the role this time, I thought, 'What can I do with it?' with the exception of looking at him and thinking that perhaps somewhere down the line he left something in my head, or my soul, or my mind that enlightened me somewhat. (My character) is very vulnerable to a line that Spock may throw at him at any time that would set him up again. But, I tried to give the impression that maybe McCoy had mellowed a little bit," Kelley explains.

Star Trek went off the air in 1967 and did not reappear as a movie until 1979. For many years it seemed that the series was dead and few cared. Yet somehow a groundswell of support was growing for the series. Kelley says, "It came to my attention around '74. I was invited to a convention in New York City which was the second one that was ever held. The first one was for about 30 people who had just liked **Star Trek** to get together in New York and something like 150 or 200 showed up. So they held another convention in New York which I was invited to attend, and they expected around 500 or 600. 10,000 people showed up. When I walked out on the stage, they let them in and the ballroom would only hold so many people. I saw them call the fire department to clear the aisles, and they were hanging from the balcony. I went home and I told my wife, 'I don't know what's going to happen with **Star Trek**, but,' I said, '*something* down the line is going to happen with this show, whether it involves us or not.' That was my first indication that they couldn't go on and on without doing something about it, and I'm absolutely astounded that Paramount didn't do something about it much earlier. I think if one of the executives had been in our shoes during some of those personal appearances, there would have been earlier action on it. They refused to do anything about it for years because they didn't want to make new episodes that would have been in competition with the syndication. After all, we were not receiving residuals for the show, so it was all gross for Paramount."

Eventually the studio executives gave the go-ahead for a movie, but the first one disappointed many fans as well as the cast. "The second movie showed that perhaps we might be back on track somewhere, because number one wasn't what any of us had in mind for a **Star Trek** movie," Kelley notes. "I wish that number four had been number one. *That's* the kind of a movie we wanted. Not necessarily that much comedy, but a human story with very few special effects is what we did an awful lot on the series. **Star Trek II** was the first spark. I don't think we had too much chance to enhance the characters, so to speak. We were too busy just trying to do a decent **Star Trek**.

"**Star Trek** was always a show concerning people, and the things that happened around them. After **Star Wars** was released, I was asked by Gene Roddenberry, what kind of a show I would like to see for (the first movie). And I said, 'Not 'City on the Edge of Forever,' but something with that feeling, which is a nice, warm, wonderful story with a minimum of special effects because (George) Lucas has done it all in **Star Wars**.' I thought it would be very refreshing to see a dynamite story come out with just a special effect here or there when it was needed; very subtle. And I wish that were the kind of thing we had done."

While **Star Trek** had the ability to guarantee an actor a part for life, it did stereotype them and deny them other outlets for their acting ability. Prior to **Star Trek**, Kelley had acted in literally dozens of movies, yet after **Star Trek** he never had another prominent role other than as the good doctor. He admits to initial resentment. "I did for a long while. I went through a period when it went into syndication and I saw that we were becoming so strongly identified with it. I had about a year of frustration. And then that's when I started to turn myself around, and I had to start thinking differently. And now I look back and think, 'Gee, I was pretty lucky to have been able to have worked in some of those marvelous films and to have done what I did, and gone on to

this.' It really doesn't bother me that much any more. I don't know why— perhaps it should. But it really doesn't."

Some people do still remember his earlier roles. "Oh, yes. In fact, I have a pair of boots on right now that I got in Lubbock, Texas when I was doing a play down there. I was signing autographs after I had performed in this play, and I looked down and I saw these cowboy boots in front of me. I looked up; There were these four cowboys and a cowgirl, and they said, 'We just came to see you because of the Westerns you've done, not **Star Trek**.' And they said, 'We own a Western store here, and we have a ranch, and we'd like to have you come in and pick out a pair of boots.' These boots came from those cowboys. I went out to the ranch, rode a horse, barbecues . . . had a wonderful time. I receive a lot of mail requesting Western stills, and Eddie Egan, in fact, had several hundred Western stills made up for me several months ago that I mail out continually. It's kinda weird. It's kinda like being stuck back in time again."

Kelley first began playing heavies for Westerns when "a director that I grew up with in Long Beach was directing some **You Were There**'s that Walter Cronkite was doing, and he said, 'De, I'm going to do a Western.. Up until that time I hadn't been doing psychopaths, ne'er do wells or the young drunkard in a rich family or that sort of thing on television. And he said, 'I want you to play a heavy for me. I think it'll be real fun for you to do it.' I said, 'What's the name of the show?' He said, 'We're going to do a documentary on Gunfight at OK Corral.' So I went out and I got all fitted up for this thing. They put a handlebar moustache on me, and I got myself a wad of tobacco and tried to make this guy a real snake. And that's how I got the motion picture. That set it off. And I just couldn't get out of them. I was there until I got into **Star Trek**.

"I enjoy playing heavies. I always enjoyed playing heavies, because I felt they were some very interesting characters. It got to be a guessing game, because I was always fearful that he'd be killed too soon and I needed the money. There're very few of them where I didn't die in some wicked way.

"I enjoyed them and they were a lot of fun to play. At the time I was doing them, there was kind of a group with Lee Van Cleef and Jack Elam —with the crazy eye— and Jim Coburn. There were about six of us that were going from show to show, and after the gunfight thing, why, I became the clean-cut heavy. He would look at you and smile, but he'd kill you at the same time."

Kelley always enjoyed Westerns more than science fiction, even after **Star Trek.** Kelley says, "It didn't stimulate my interest because I never had any interest in science fiction. I really couldn't have cared less about it, and I had seen very little. It was really not my cup of tea. I'm not a buff. I don't sit and read science fiction as such. I enjoyed the science fiction that we did. I had to 'get' the science fiction to do the show. But I'm not a science fiction addict by any means.

"I enjoyed the stories that we did in **Star Trek**, and I learned very much to like it; my wife doesn't to this day."

COMMUN ICATIONS

OFFICER

Nyota was the younger child of a computer analyst and a professor of Terran literature at the University of Nairobi in Kenya, one of the states of the United States of Africa. Nyota's parents trained both of their children in Swahili. Nyota picked it up easily.

Nyota also quickly learned to read, and began devouring her father's collection of off-world literature in his study. Through these books, Nyota loved to study all the facets of different cultures. The complexity of other societies and their similarities and differences from her own intrigued her.

Nyota's brother, Kamal, was several years older than she, and was already attending the University studying his own native Bantu tribal culture, in hopes of becoming an envoy for the US of Africa to the United Nations.

Nyota developed into an exceptionally intelligent child. She showed a natural aptitude for languages, and became fluent in Fed-Standard, old French, ancient Gaelic, and increasingly, in Vulcan, by her teen years. For being born into a highly technological society, however, she was particularly technology shy. It was hard for her to become comfortable with the simplest computerized tutors in her school.

"To say I could hardly even punch up my breakfast in the morning wasn't far from the truth. My mother, the computer wonder, really was supportive. She got me interested in the puzzle-solving aspects of computers, and that kept me intrigued. I loved to break codes and ciphers, and I think that helped me warm up to them at least," Nyota said.

Her brother Kamal gained more notoriety as he completed advanced work at the University and joined the Kenyan representatives in the African delegation to the U.N. Nyota respected her brother's work and achievements, but she preferred to concentrate on other societies and to learn as much of the diversity of the galaxy as possible. She wanted to visit those other societies and unite everyone in their diversity. "The Bantu have a beautiful culture, one that I am proud to be a part of, but I want to go beyond one culture. Everyone has a different culture, and each one is beautiful. I want to be a part of that," said Nyota.

As she entered maturity, others found Nyota as strikingly beautiful as she was intelligent. She easily passed her mastery test of the Vulcan tongue. Even with the popularity she gained in school because of both her good looks and keen intelligence, she was always "Kamal's younger sister." He had become widely known as a powerful statesman, pushing harder and harder to develop Africa's trade relations. "Kamal was certainly charismatic. My friends, the tribespeople, even his professors at the University, were all pulled in and enthralled by my brother's oration.

"I didn't feel it consciously, no one was being too obvious about it, but I felt second best to Kamal since I can remember. Not only was everyone enchanted by him, but he also pulled me on his coattails for a while until I jumped off," said Nyota.

PROFILE

Nyota accepted the challenge in high school to evolve her own self and break away from Kamal's shadow. "The biggest shock to my teachers was that I wasn't as gallant as my brother. Everything was in flowing strokes for Kamal, everything was grand, and very noble. His speech was like music. I do have to thank Kamal for my voice. He was the one who truly taught me to speak when I was very young. Aside from that, he was very stately, and I was always very direct. Kamal loved debate, and he did it well and honorably. On the other hand, while I enjoyed a good discussion, I would tell someone where to get off if they were truly bothering me," said Nyota.

Soon everyone at school looked at her with respect, but a different sort of respect than they had shown her older brother. Where her school officials admired Kamal for his inspiration, they admired his sister for her decisiveness. Where Kamal had made great inspirational speeches, Nyota inspired people for what she did, especially with her work to establish an exchange program between students from Kenya and non-Terran students. She gained her popularity by including everyone in what tasks needed to be done, and she did more of the work herself to help other people. Nyota graduated from her high school both with academic achievement honors and the highest respect from her peers for her hands-on leadership.

A scholarship awaited her at the University of Nairobi. Several professors wanted her to pursue academic research on non-Terran cultures to add to the body of Terran knowledge. Nyota turned this down. "I would much rather get out there first hand to meet these non-Terrans as real people. I want to learn about them, and I want them to learn about me. I want to make the galaxy a less scary and a more friendly place," said Nyota in her letter to the dean of the University in which she declined the scholarship.

Instead she immediately applied to Starfleet Academy. Getting in wasn't easy. Nyota travelled to San Francisco with her parents for a day of exhausting academic and personal tests. She scored consistently high and was ecstatic when Starfleet accepted her. There would be no better place for actual live contact and cultural exchange with alien worlds than in Starfleet. Also, Starfleet had a certain prestige attached to it. Even to be accepted into the Academy was a big deal. Kamal had made his mark; Nyota was determined to make hers.

Once again Nyota helped people and exhibited the natural leadership she had practiced in high school at the Academy. Cadet Uhura quickly became exceptionally prominent to her superiors for her leadership in academics, intercultural work, and for revamping the Starfleet Choir. The other cadets and faculty learned quickly of Nyota's exceptional voice. She was the soloist at many Starfleet Academy ceremonies. She also performed at Starfleet Command once for Fleet Admiral Nogura's retirement ceremony.

With her skills in language and her experience playing code-breaking on computers in her childhood, she decided that she would concentrate on Communications. It would be the optimum way to gain first contact privileges with alien cultures. She exemplified herself in her classes, especially her Communications classes. Nyota picked up codes easily, as well as communications protocols.

She graduated after three years, and was assigned to the *USS Regulus* as an assistant communications officer. For a year Nyota's duties aboard the *Regulus* consisted mainly of routine ship-to-planetside communications, as well as a few decodings of Starfleet Command transmissions. While the other cadet communication officers struggled, Nyota breezed through, working efficiently, and helping the other cadets when she got a chance.

After the *Regulus* returned to Earth, the cadet cruise finished, Nyota faced a difficult choice. As a new ensign, she had the opportunity to enter Command School. In fact, her cadet commander had recommended her for it. However, Ensign Nyota wanted to get into deep space as quickly as possible. The *Regulus* had stayed within the confines of settled Federation space, and while Nyota indeed enjoyed the exposure to non-Terran Federation races, she was truly looking forward to contact with new races. That's where the key to a peaceful galaxy lay, Nyota believed.

Nyota opted out of Command School, but decided to attend at some later point. Starfleet assigned her aboard the *USS Tremaine*, a frigate, as chief communications officer. The *Tremaine*, while not probing as deeply into space as perhaps the heavy cruisers would, did venture into unexplored space. It was the *Tremaine* who first made Federation contact with the mysterious Tholian Assembly during this voyage. Nyota knew that her skill at communications was crucial in not only keeping her ship from being destroyed, but also in avoiding full conflict with the Tholians.

There was some exchange of fire between the Tholians and the *Tremaine*, which knocked out several systems, including communications. It was crippling to the establishment of good relations between the two powers. The *Tremaine*'s captain, wanted communication restored immediately to avoid a devastating war. Nyota called for the techs to fix her panel. When they didn't arrive soon enough, she dived under the equipment thrusting her hands in the electronic innards, repairing the system herself. "I had truly begun working before I knew what I was doing. Had this been less than life and death, I would have frozen in my fear of computer systems. But as it was, my nature told me it needed doing, so I did it. And I had the panel back on-line within minutes," Nyota later said. Her captain commended her for technical talent and initiative.

After *Tremaine*'s three year mission, Nyota had accrued enough commendations for her captain to sponsor her promotion to full lieutenant. But once again, there was a choice. Again, the offer stood of Command School. But Captain James T. Kirk had read reports of the Tholian incident, including the captain of the *Tremaine*'s report on outstanding staff during the incident. Kirk was looking to assemble a crew of the top officers in each field for his ship, the *Enterprise*. Nyota Uhura was clearly the best communications officer. She leapt at the opportunity for an intensive five year mission aboard a heavy cruiser, a mission whose primary purpose would be to contact alien life and explore new worlds.

Born in Robbins, Illinois, Nichelle's father served as both town mayor and chief magistrate. At the age of sixteen she wrote a ballet for a musical suite by Duke Ellington.

A brilliant dancer and a fine singer, Nichelle demonstrated her ability as an actress by twice being nominated for the Sara Siddon Award as best actress of the year. Her first nomination was for her portrayal of Hazel Sharp in "Kicks and Co.," the second for her performance in the hit play, "The Blacks."

Born and raised in Chicago, she studied there as well as in New York and Los Angeles. During her time in New York, she appeared at both the famed Blue Angel and the Playboy Club. Between appearances at the clubs, she doubled as standby and understudy to the lead in the Broadway musical, "No Strings." She appeared in the title role of a Chicago stock company production of "Carmen Jones."

On the West Coast, Nichelle appeared in "Roar of the Grease Paint, Smell of the Crowd" and "For My People" and won high critical acclaim for her performance in the James Baldwin play, "Blues for Mr. Charlie."

As vocalist with the Duke Ellington and Lionel Hampton bands, she toured throughout the United States, Canada and Europe.

Although a stage veteran, Nichelle was a relatively new face to television at the time **Star Trek** began filming in the Sixties. Previously she had only appeared in **The Lieutenant** (also produced by Gene Roddenberry) and as the lead in an episode of **CBS Repertory Theatre**. While the latter was closer to her previous experience, it was on **The Lieutenant** that she was spotted by Gene Roddenberry and tapped for the role of Lt. Uhura.

She appeared in the films **Mister Buddwing, Three for the Wedding, Truck Turner, Made in Paris, Porgy and Bess** (where she danced with Sammy Davis, Jr.) and **Doctor You've Got To Be Kidding**.

Following the cancellation of **Star Trek** in 1969 she returned to the night club circuit. Before **Star Trek** she had toured with Duke Ellington and the Lionel Hampton bands throughout the United States, Canada and Europe. During the Seventies she released a single, "Shoop Shoop," on 20th Century Records and often sang at her many appearances at **Star Trek** conventions. She released an album, "Dark Side of the Moon," through Americana Records.

During her leisure hours, Nichelle enjoys oil painting, designing her own clothes, sports cars, reading science fiction, writing and sculpting.

Nichelle is still active professionally, and performed the voice for Lt. Uhura for the **Star Trek** animated series as well as appearing in all five of the **Star Trek** motion pictures. She has also acted as spokesperson for her favorite charity, "The Kwanza Foundation."

Nichelle became involved with the space program when she flew aboard the C-141 Astronomy Observatory (which analyzed the atmospheres of Mars and Saturn), on an eight hour, high altitude mission. She was a special guest at the

THE ACTOR

Jet Propulsion Laboratory in Pasadena on July 17, 1976 to view the Viking probe's soft landing on Mars. Nichelle wrote about the Viking mission for a publication of the National Space Institute. She joined the Space Shuttle astronaut recruitment program after giving a speech to the Board of Directors of the National Space Institute on "New Opportunities for the Humanization of Space," which dealt with the lack of women and minorities in the space program. Along with many of the other cast members from the original **Star Trek** series, she attended the launching at Cape Canaveral of the first space shuttle, which was of course named *The Enterprise*.

By Dennis Fischer

The jobs of the major characters aboard the starship *Enterprise* are easy to understand because we often see them performing their tasks. The Captain runs things while Spock mans the readouts at the science station. Chekov navigates while Sulu acts as helmsman and Scotty makes certain his "poor bairns" don't overheat. We know that Lt. Uhura opens the hailing frequencies because she gets the opportunity to tell us so often. Her function as communications officer is obscured because we don't see her monitoring the various bands while routing important calls to their proper places within the ship. After battle stations, when damage reports come in, it is Uhura who quickly and expertly assesses the information to report on damages to Captain Kirk.

The job is far more than the space-faring switchboard operator some have dubbed it. Ably played by Nichelle Nichols, Uhura was largely kept in the background through most of the series. There are some **Star Trek** moments which are clearly hers. Who can forget her scene with the black crewman in "The Man Trap?" Her response to Sulu's dubbing her a "fair maiden" ("Sorry, neither!") in "The Naked Time?" Her near-rape in "The Gamesters of Triskelion?" Her sexy come-on to the alternate universe Sulu in "Mirror, Mirror?" Her vision of Captain Kirk in "The Tholian Web" and television's first interracial kiss in "Plato's Stepchildren?" About the latter, Nichols says that kissing Shatner was "very difficult. We had to do 36 takes." Laughing, she adds, "Somehow, it didn't bother us at all."

In **Star Trek III**, she had a delightful scene in which she held a bored cadet, listed in the credits as "Mr. Fantasy," at phaserpoint to allow Kirk and his crew to beam aboard and abscond with the Enterprise. Joining the renegade crew on Vulcan, she restated her loyalty confirming her position as a permanent part of the **Star Trek** family.

The multitalented Nichols heralds from Chicago. "I'm Spanish, Welsh, African and Cherokee Indian," she explains. "My parents had two mixes each. I guess everybody in America is one kind of mixture or another.

"I've always known what I wanted to do and what I wanted to be. I studied ballet, all the forms of dance, acting and singing. I was dancing somewhere in Chicago when Duke Ellington came through town and saw me. I was sixteen and he took me on tour with his band. I would say that was my first big break. I'd been doing plays and singing and dancing, so I guess I'd been preparing for that one. Things went on from there. One part led to another and here I am."

Nichols has been nominated for the Sara Siddons Award for best actress of the year twice (for the plays "The Blacks" and "Kicks and Company"). Her films include **Doctor, You've Got To Be Kidding, Made in Paris, Mr. Buddwing, Porgy and Bess, Three for the Wedding, Truck Turner** and **The Supernatural**, in which she stars as Sergeant Leona Hawkins.

INTERVIEW

Nichols very nearly missed appearing in **Star Trek** altogether. "I was in Europe when my manager sent me a telegram that said, 'Come back here, doing **Star Trek**'," she recalls. "I had decided to stay in Europe for a long time, though, so I didn't answer him. He tracked me down in Paris and sent me a ticket and a note that read, 'It's a round trip, first class, and if you don't get the job the ticket's on me.' That was an offer I couldn't refuse, so I came back and read for the part, and I got it. My manager just felt it was absolutely right for me."

Nichols likes all of the **Star Trek** films. "I like the first film, although I felt it wasn't **Star Trek**. If you go back and see it, you'll find that it's an exciting science fiction movie which simply had the characters of **Star Trek**. But it didn't have the essence of what **Star Trek** really was. I think that with all of us being away from it for so long, there wasn't the sense of family and unity, of camaraderie, between the main characters, as there was in the series. That was captured in the second movie, and certainly in the third."

Star Trekker Nichelle Nichols continues to do a lot of work for NASA. Recently, she received NASA's highest award for her years of service to the organization. She is particularly proud that she was under contract to them to recruit the first woman astronauts for the space shuttle program, as well as the first black and ethnic astronauts. "The first women you see now going up are the women that I assisted in recruiting back in 1977; the first black man that you see is from that recruitment," she recalls proudly.

Her work with NASA continues. "Right now I've accepted a position on the board of directors of the Young Astronauts Program, which was created by Jack Anderson in Washington, D.C.. It is run under the auspices of the executive branch and is headquartered out of the White House. I will be heading up the celebrity section, the 'Guiding Stars' we're calling ourselves. I'll be coordinating the celebrities to support and work. This is for young people in elementary school. We're making them aware of what the space program does for us, its many benefits and the possibilities of their being astronauts themselves. We're also preparing them educationally for the space age technology and careers that we're really just beginning to appreciate."

Nichols also continues to be active in her singing career. She's recorded an album, "Out of This World" and a single, "Beyond Antares" backed with "Uhura's Theme."

"Currently I'm recording a video album, which I'm very excited about, of beautiful music written by my partner Jim Meechan, which he's producing. It's music with a space theme. Some of it is ballad, some of it is rock and some of it is almost country/ western. But it's very space-oriented and it's called "Future Trekking."

Like other **Star Trek** celebrities, Nichols has also been involved in a couple of writing projects. Sondra Marshak and Myrna Culbreath wrote the story "Surprise!" based on Nichols' idea in *Star Trek: The New Voyages 2*. Comments Nichols, "I gave them the idea and they wrote it up. It was . . . okay." Nichols also has plans to write a book for which she is still putting material together.

Reflecting on what made **Star Trek** so popular and appealing, Nichols offers these thoughts, "I think that it came at a time when there was a lot of strife in the world. Not that there isn't now, but that was when we had Vietnam and the flower children and young people experimenting with narcotics and mind-expanding drugs. There was a lot of thwarting of authority and the status quo of living and dying. I think **Star Trek** gave hope for the future. There was also a feeling that we were going to self-destruct back then. That we were going to annihilate ourselves with the atom bomb and nuclear power.

"**Star Trek** said to us, 'Not only are you going to survive into the 23rd century, but you will go to the stars and on missions of peaceful exploration with an edict of non-interference.' Not only did Gene (Roddenberry) do that, but I think it said we would all be there, men and women of all colors, on an equal basis. Our aims in life were of the highest order as opposed to the **Star Wars** mentality, which can be summed up in how big and badly can we blow it up and how fast. The **Star Trek** mentality is for the progress and development of the future, seeking science and knowledge.

"**Star Trek** said to us that we are not victims of our technology. We were not lost in space. Our technology was developed and is used much as our technology is today. As supersonic jets have the power to move from here to Europe in a few hours, we were able to move from star to star. We've conquered the mysteries of propulsion and interstellar travel. I think it also showed that our technology is an extension of our own intelligence. It's not something that is a destructive force. It was used as a positive, constructive force.

"I also think it did not make robots or humanoids of us, or make us superior. We were the same people with the same foibles, ideas, ambitions, fears and pain as people have in this day and age. We're the ancestors of all the new generations and those generations are only going to be as good or as bad as we make them. How high we set our ideals today will determine how our posterity performs in the future."

That the perception of women's roles has changed in the last 20 years is plain in the following anecdote. While recording her lines for the animated episode, "The Lorelei Signal", Nichols came across a line in which Uhura announces that she's taking over the ship. " 'What!'," Nichols exclaims, " 'She gets to take over the ship!' I couldn't believe it! But then I was furious because we had to do it in animation.

"In the series, before they would turn it over to a woman, they would turn it over to someone who was below my rank. It didn't bother me so much as it bothered my fans. They were the people who wrote in, especially women, of course. It didn't bother me because it was an acting job. I wasn't involved in rank and what it looked like. But the fans were and that was very interesting. It meant a great deal, too. However, that was corrected in the films,

although not with me. (Lt. Saavik takes over in **Wrath of Khan**.) Certainly women were in control of the ship, but that was 1965.

"You know, I was the only woman on the command deck, and I was the only woman on the command crew. Whenever they need that other side—the flip of a coin—of the heroism of Captain Kirk and the mystic strength of Mr. Spock, the writers thought who better than to have our poor Uhura saying, 'I'm frightened, Captain.'"

Lieutenant Uhura has finally been given a first name. Says Nichols, "Someone has written a book about the history of **Star Trek** and he decided to give her a first name. It's 'Nyoka' which I think is very beautiful. In Swahili, it means 'star'. Of course, 'Uhura' is a made-up word we took from the Swahili word 'Uhuru,' which means freedom. Gene softened the end of it from a 'u' to an 'a'... Uhura."

There are many aspects of Uhura's personality that Nichols would one day like to see developed. "I'd like to show her personal side. What are her ambitions and aims? Her lovelife and her family life? What makes her the one person that is chosen by Starfleet to go on this historic five year mission as Communications Officer? What made her capable beyond anyone else? How did she devel op into the woman she is now and what makes her the proud, strong woman that she is?

"Probably most important, I would love to see the personal side of her, what she cares about. I think that I portrayed her as a strong, silent type, quiet but firm, yet compassionate. Intelligent and feminine at the same time. These are the characteristics that I wanted to give her. A sense of dignity and honesty and strength, while still being feminine and having compassion and emotions like any other human being."

Over the years as **Star Trek** has gone into syndication, bits and pieces have been cut from each episode to make room for more and more commercials. Often these bits would feature Uhura, so when the newly struck prints were released from Paramount many fans were delighted to see these scenes reinstated.

Says Nichols, "It's thanks to the fans. They began to write in and protest the cuts, especially those cuts that I'm in. They started writing in to sponsors and they had a little coalition and protest faction, which 'shows to go you' that sponsors do listen to their customers. Then the fans wrote in when the scenes were restored and thanked the sponsors and told them they would buy their products. I think that's pretty good clout.

"The great thing about **Star Trek** is the fans. It proves that what Gene created, that which came from his heart about a better world to live in, was seen, heard and appreciated. It was supported and refused to let die. And it lives today, which again I think just proves that positive, constructive forces are more powerful than destructive, negative ones.

"I'm delighted with it, and I'm delighted that so many people see it that way and feel that way about it. I'm very proud of it and that I have some small part in effecting that."

THE
ENGINEER

Ever since he was a "wee lad," as his father Ian called him, Montgomery Scott was tinkering with something. Montgomery grew up on a sheep farm outside of Aberdeen, Scotland. As a child, Montgomery had two favorite pastimes: playing with the family's big sheepdog, Duke, and fixing things and watching other people fix things.

After Montgomery was born, Duke more and more became the boy's pet rather than the family sheepdog, and Duke would follow Montgomery wherever the boy went. As a very young boy, Montgomery would run in the fields with Duke, trying to ride the dog, making up complex adventures. As Montgomery got older, Duke began to follow him to school, and waited for him at the end of the day.

After school, Montgomery tinkered out in the shed. He started with simple mechanical farm implements, taking them apart one piece at a time, studying each component, what they did separately, and what they did as part of the whole. Then he would put them back together. Duke often sat up in one corner to watch Montgomery work, and Montgomery enjoyed the audience.

As he got a little older, Montgomery started working on larger things, like computers and his father's hovercraft. Montgomery was quite patient. If he couldn't figure something out immediately, he might curse and bellow a bit in frustration, but he would let it sit and mull it over in his mind and go back to it later. He was talented, and could figure out most gadgets relatively easily. Soon Montgomery was getting the bulk of his education by himself. He learned advanced physics concepts, mathematical theory, and the origins of logic long before his classmates. He augmented his practical work out in the shed with curiosity-satisfying trips to the Aberdeen library to put the ideas into perspective.

It came as little surprise to his family that Montgomery did well in school, and exceptionally well in math and the theoretical sciences. He also showed an interest in ancient Gaelic culture, picking up a set of bagpipes for his fifteenth birthday. In his spare time, Montgomery practiced the bagpipes while reading vidisplays of technical manuals.

Montgomery joined the Aberdeen Marching Band, playing the bagpipes. The band played all over the Earth and the Federation for various state ceremonies and parades.Ian and Montgomery's mother Mary were proud of their son, although Ian almost had a heart attack the day he went out to find his son puttering with the farm's private generator. Montgomery stood in the middle of enough current to turn his tartan kilt black. Ian found Montgomery upgrading the generator to produce a cleaner power flow.

Although Montgomery spent much of his time buried in technical pursuits, he also found plenty of occasion for old-fashioned carousing. He would go out with his friends Duncan, Sean, and Alan and head into Aberdeen after school. Ian passed down the secrets of distillery to his son, and Montgomery kept a still in his work shed. The boys always went into town with a bottle or two of

PROFILE

good quality family Scotch. Once in town, they picked up a female or two a piece, and would joyride in Duncan's hovercar.

Montgomery beguiled many a woman with winning charm. Too free-spirited to hang on to one particular lass, he enjoyed chasing several.

Montgomery dreamed of adventure, but fell in love with generators and computer systems. He loved them more than any woman he knew in Aberdeen. Because of his high scores on math and physics aptitude tests, Montgomery was offered scholarships to many engineering universities sponsored by astroflight corporations with high paying development positions available to him upon graduation.

Montgomery was familiar with commercial spaceflight, and the "piddling developments" that were made there, as he put it. "Those clunkers couldn't get out of molasses for anything," Montgomery said. He wanted to be where the real challenges lay, in Starfleet. Starfleet was then embarking on an aggressive development plan for a series of new heavy cruisers that would go faster for longer periods of time than any other in history. "Those lassies'll really go places," Montgomery said.

Upon entrance into Starfleet Academy, Montgomery sank into any and all available manuals on Starfleet technology, including plans for the new Constitution class ships. "Smoother than a shot of old Scotch," Montgomery said in his best brogue.

His classmates were fascinated with the new Scottish cadet who wore his lucky kilt to exams. The women loved his honey-warm brogue, and listened to him spin yarns of the Scottish highlands for hours. All the cadets eagerly noted Montgomery's age-old recipe for Scotch, which the engineering cadets happily used to improve the quality of their "engine-room hooch," crude moonshine that Montgomery's recipe and expert touch made so much better. The cadets also loved Montgomery's exciting flair for the Scottish ways, and nicknamed the friendly chap "Scotty." Whether it was a class taught by the Academy's most pedantic instructor, or a night pass into San Francisco, Scotty made sure he enlivened it for his peers. They all became his friends. Scotty took his engineering seriously, but took the engineer with a grain of salt.

In his last year at Academy, Scotty opted for advanced engineering work on the Constitution ships, eventually contributing the dilithium flow design to the plans. For his exceptional work as a cadet, the dean of engineering commended Scotty by sponsoring him for a promotion to full ensign, and ordered that Scotty's cadet cruise would be to help supervise the *Constitution*'s shakedown cruise.

For two years he was aboard for the full shakedown, a year longer than traditional cadet cruises. Scotty watched every systems monitor aboard ship, especially tending to the dilithium, fiddling with his original plans occasionally, retooling the cut of the crystals for maximum efficiency for such a large ship that ran a huge number of systems. Scotty loved feeling he had contributed something. He learned that if he wasn't constantly on demand to produce a hundred different engineering miracles at once, he felt useless, which he hated.

Scotty didn't get much of the adventure he had dreamed of as a child because Starfleet didn't completely trust the new ship, yet. But he was eventually given the chance to proudly say that with only a few minor reworkings, *Constitution* and her sisters were the best the Federation had. Scotty felt a warm spot when he realized he was lumped in with the distinguished Federation minds.

After the *Constitution* mission, Starfleet offered to let Scotty remain with the *Constitution* to supervise a minor refit, then ship out with her again. Parts of the Constitution had already slipped into near-obsolescence. The state-of-the-art at that very moment was the glistening new *Enterprise*.

The *Enterprise* had just completed a scaled-down version of the *Constitution* shakedown under Captain Robert April who was moving on to the Federation diplomatic corps. Captain Christopher Pike was taking over as commander for a full five year mission. This was the chance for Montgomery Scott to not only serve aboard the most current advanced ship, but to enter actual deep space. Scotty beamed at the opportunity for a little starhopping adventure.

He transferred on as assistant chief engineering officer, lieutenant junior grade. The *Enterprise* made Scotty even prouder than the *Constitution*. The *Enterprise* was one of those rare ships with personality. "From Day One, she was a gallant lady," said Scotty later in life. Scotty served two five year missions under Pike, followed by a six month refit he supervised while his chief engineering officer went on maternity leave.

She resigned from the service before the second five year cruise, and Scotty then served under Clegg Pitcairn, an old engineer who had been one of the supervisors of the *Constitution* design team. After the second five years, which included the infamous Talos incident, Commander Pitcairn went into retirement.

Once again, Scotty supervised a refit, but this time in his own right, as he had been promoted from lieutenant to lieutenant commander and given the job of chief engineer. "Accepting that promotion was a true marriage to the *Enterprise*. It was sick or poor, 'til death do us part. And that's how it was," said Scotty later.

With the promotion and refit, came a mostly new crew. Pike and his exec, Number One, were gone. Captain James T. Kirk came aboard as skipper. Scotty sized him up another man who loved his ship, and true to his belief, Kirk never asked more from the old girl than she could give.

Scotty had found that too many people think of starships as pieces of technology to bully around. To Scotty the *Enterprise* was different. Treat her with care, and she'll look after you forever.

A native of Vancouver, British Columbia, Doohan earned the name "bad boy" while flying an artillery observation plane during World War II for the Royal Canadian Air Force. Concerning this, Doohan says, "I guess they thought I was crazy because I used to fly my plane on a slalom course through rows of telephone poles." Prior to this he had been wounded in battle on D-Day.

James Doohan first came to the United States in 1946 on a two-year scholarship to the Neighborhood Playhouse in New York City where he continued on as a teacher for three years, teaching acting techniques at New York City's Neighborhood Playhouse. In 1953 he returned to Toronto, Canada, where he lived for the next eight years. During this time he appeared in more than four hundred live and taped television shows, numerous motion pictures and plays, as well as over three thousand radio shows.

Prior to securing the role of Chief Engineer Scott on Star Trek, Doohan had appeared on such TV shows as **Bonanza, Hazel, The Virginian, Blue Light, Daniel Boone, The F.B.I., The Gallant Men, Gunsmoke** and **The Man from U.N.C.L.E.** Other guest appearances for television were for **The Outer Limits, Peyton Place, Return to Peyton Place, Shenandoah, Then Came Bronson, The Twilight Zone, Voyage to the Bottom of the Sea, The Fugitive, Iron Horse, Ben Casey, Bewitched,** and a recurring part on Jason of Star Command from 1978 to '79.

His many motion picture credits include **The Wheeler Dealers, Fellowship, Jigsaw, The Satan Bug, Bus Riley's Back in Town, Pretty Maids All in a Row** and **Man in the Wilderness.** He also appeared in several films produced by the National Film Board of Canada.

At the same time he read for the role of Scotty on **Star Trek** he was also under consideration for the role of the chief engineer on **Voyage to the Bottom of the Sea.** He would have have received that part if **Star Trek** had not come through first.

An expert dialectician, Doohan has provided voices for many cartoons and commercial characters. In the **Star Trek** cartoon series he did the voice of Scotty as well as those of several other characters, including one for the episode "Yesteryear" when he was the voice of both The Guardian and of Spock's father.

On November 22, 1967, Doohan married his second wife, the former Anita Yagel, a secretary employed by Paramount whom he met in the studio commissary. He has four children by a previous marriage.

An accomplished carpenter and wood carver, James Doohan has made several pieces of furniture which the Doohans use in their Hollywood Hills residence.

Besides appearing in all five of the **Star Trek** motion pictures, Doohan has performed occasional guest shots, such as on **Magnum P.I.** where he played a Scotsman!

THE ACTOR

By Thomas Pratt

"Ladies and gentlemen, your favorite engineer and mine, James (Scotty) Doohan!"

And with that the small, jam-packed auditorium exploded into thunderous applause as our favorite Scotsman casually strolled to center stage and proclaimed, "Welcome to Friday Night Live!" From that moment on the fans were his and he would have their undivided attention for the rest of the evening.

He paused for a moment before asking if there were any engineers in the audience. Doohan explained, "I consider myself an engineer. I always have ever since I was about eight when I built naval ships with rubber band paddles, and every time it rained I had a ball having naval battles." With this the crowd again broke into laughter.

After this delightful opening, Doohan switched to a more serious topic. He stated that the film we were about to see was very dear to his heart and was also, in his opinion, very important to us all as it dealt with the possible future of mankind. The title of the film was **Universe**, and it was narrated by his friend and on-screen captain William Shatner.

Universe is a short film dealing with the origin of the universe, evolution and other fascinating aspects of existence. The story is told through the utilization of incredible animation techniques combined with a fine musical soundtrack. But it's William Shatner's narration that makes it work. He takes the audience on an amazing voyage into space to see the incredible vastness and beauty of our universe. Shatner shows us black holes and the origin and death of stars, as well as information about the planets in our own solar system. It was easy to see why James Doohan recommended the film so highly and with such personal enthusiasm.

When the film ended, Doohan returned to the stage to discuss NASA, and explained the reason he shows the film. "We are the people, we are the generation, that is starting the trek to other galaxies, to other planets, and that is why NASA needs your support. NASA is a tremendous organization and they don't do anything without making damn sure it is going to work." He explained that a lot of people believe that he gets paid for promoting NASA, but of course NASA is one of our governmental agencies and they can't pay him. He doesn't really care. "I do it for the love of country, for love of the future, and for love of you. I just want you to think about it any time we have something that NASA needs some support on, because we are the people who are the best pioneers in the world for the future, because our future generations are going to have to get out there somewhere—whether they do it in space colonies millions of miles away from Earth, or on another planet, and meet with other, let's hope, human beings. I certainly don't think we are going to run

INTERVIEW

into many monsters that are going to stand up on their hind legs and look like lizards and talk English." (Referring, of course, to the Gorns in the **Star Trek** episode "Arena.")

Following his views on the future of mankind in space, Mr. Doohan introduced the blooper film which, according to him, would warm us up for the rest of the evening. (The **Star Trek** blooper reel is one of those permanent classics in fandom, a hilarious collection of out-takes from the daily filming of the television series. It was originally edited for Gene Roddenberry to use at private parties.)

Before the final segment of the evening, the question and answer period, began, Doohan chose to answer a few of the questions people were always asking. The first question was from people who had bought the *Star Trek Technical Manual*. They wanted to know why there were no drawings for toilets. Doohan's explanation was simply, "I told them that we do have phasers, and you set them on disintegrate, and aim, very, very carefully."

The second most asked question concerned how he got the Scotty role. He explained that it was because he does a lot of different accents. He'd read for a show two weeks before landing **Star Trek** in which the part called for a Scotland Yard inspector. Although he didn't get that role, ten days later the director, who also happened to be the director for the **Star Trek** pilot, called him up and asked him to come down and do some of his accents. He went down to read for them one morning and they handed him a page from the script. Doohan read it in five or six different accents, and got the part as Chief Engineer Montgomery Scott.

Then it was the audience's turn to ask the questions.

One curious member of the audience asked why the Klingons have in the movies have the bone ridge on their head while in the television series they don't.

Doohan responded, "Before I found out the real answer, I used to say that it's because I sent the tribbles over to them and that's what the tribbles did to them. But the real reason was that in the big motion picture, they didn't want any alien to look too much like humans. So that's what they came out with and that's the official answer.

Another member of the audience inquired why Scotty always tells Captain Kirk he couldn't get the extra power the captain demanded and then always did.

In his Scottish accent brogue, Doohan explained, "That's because ah noo how ta git the power!"

One perceptive member of the audience asked Doohan if acting in the **Star Trek** television series changed the way industry people tended to perceived him as an actor, and whether it changed the way he perceived himself.

"No, it certainly hasn't changed my perception of who I am," Doohan responded. He continued, "However you must forgive Hollywood in their ignorance. They do tend to typecast, and unfortunately, in the past ten years, except for (the Star Trek films) there has been only one part for a Scotsman. So I've had to go to Europe and Canada, the stage and so on and play other characters than Scotsmen. The only Scotsman I ever played before in my life was in one episode of **Hazel** in 1962. But then again, you look at it and you have to say to yourself, Well, so you're not getting to work in Hollywood, but you're famous, right?"

THE
HELMSMAN

Although Hikaru Sulu was born in Hawaii to Isao and Mitsuko Sulu, both of Japanese heritage, young Hikaru never saw much of his birthplace. His parents, a botanist and a poet, moved to agricultural station Wexler VIII early in Hikaru's life. His mother, the botanist, researched ways to yield larger protein ratios in crop harvests on thin-atmosphere marginal class M worlds.

His father became one of the better-known poets of the Federation, writing frequently about Wexler VIII, a planet of extreme contrasts. Because of its positioning near two stars, and its tilt on its axis, half of the world is lush like the Sulus' homeland while the other half of the planet is a barren waste with the inhabitants living under envirodomes. All of the planet, however, was almost devoid of sentient life, which Hikaru's father Isao found peaceful and conducive to creativity.

On Wexler, Hikaru went to a Federation colony school where children from throughout the Federation attended. Young Hikaru was excited by stories of far-off planets and people, but he always dreamed of going home to the Pacific on Earth, the home he didn't remember, but his parents always talked about.

When Hikaru was nine, he and his parents left Wexler. His mother was finished with the preliminaries of her work and ready to go to thin-atmosphere planets to test it. Mitsuko hoped to finally reap agricultural benefits. The Sulus spent the next five years hopping from planet to planet. In this time, Hikaru got a better sense of space, and of direction.

"I got out there, and I realized that space was incredibly big. I dreamed a lot about piloting a spaceship out there, going to see all the places I'd heard about. I guess I wanted to steer my own life," said Hikaru.

During these travelling years, Hikaru and his parents didn't stay in one place for very long, which made Hikaru's education difficult. It also made making friends almost impossible. Spending so much time around his mother and her peers, without kids his own age to be with, Hikaru eventually took an interest in his mother's work. The lifecycle of plants fascinated him. "They live, and they seem so simple, yet like people they're very complex. You always think you've gotten to know them, but you're constantly discovering something new," Hikaru explained.

His nomadic life led Hikaru into becoming a voracious reader. He especially took a fancy to adventures such as those of Robin Hood, the Three Musketeers, and Medieval Europe in general. Hikaru eventually picked up fencing as a physical diversion in the confined spaces of an envirodome. Usually, Hikaru fenced against automated programmed drones, but when he was lucky, he would run into another fencing enthusiast.

Hikaru really let his true savvy show when he fought against another fencer. When he was competing against another person, the challenge wasn't just the reflexes and moves that a drone tested, but of his mind and spirit against another's.

PROFILE

As Hikaru grew older, he began to feel restricted in the tight confines of an envirodome. Without companions his own age, Hikaru grew restless and bored. He saw an outlet in the station's hovercraft, normally used for quick checks of the numerous seeded plots. Hikaru often took one of the station's hovercraft beyond the envirodome, seeing what he and the machine could do. Sulu never took a companion along on these excursions. He wasn't looking to show off, just to entertain himself and satisfy his curiosity in the relationship between pilot and vehicle.

Because Hikaru kept a low profile , he never was caught by the station authorities. Hikaru did innocuously volunteer to repair hovercraft after the station manager "just happened" to mention to him that hovercraft with extreme metal fatigue had been discovered. From then on, he made sure the 'craft he took out were returned in their original condition, or better.

When Hikaru was almost sixteen, his mother finished her protein yield work, and the Sulus relocated back to Wexler. Hikaru had suggested to his parents that they return to Earth, but they had grown accustomed to making the stars their home. His mother's protein yield work had been a success, so Mitsuko began working on several other projects. Hikaru was glad to settle down for more than six months at a time on a planet he was familiar with, even if he did view the prospect with boredom.

"No where in my imagination could I ever picture any swashbuckling going on on Wexler. But my boredom wasn't my worst problem. I was having trouble keeping up in my new classes on Wexler," said Hikaru.

Each time the Sulus had moved to another planet, Hikaru's curriculum had changed at least slightly, and he had never been in any one place long enough to grasp the concepts fully. Isao tutored his son to compensate, but Sulu was still uncertain when it came to academics, especially pure mathematics. Every class he had attended proved different than his last one, and he suffered large gaps in his education.

As graduation from high school approached, Hikaru gave more serious thought to his boyhood dreams of going to Japan and exploring the culture that up until now he had only experienced second-hand. Now Hikaru wanted to journey triumphantly to Japan and feast on it. Hikaru planned to study at the University of Tokyo to get a degree in botany and agriculture and eventually start a small experimental hydrofarm on one of the Japanese islands.

His parents understood their son's decision, and Isao offered to tutor Hikaru in spoken and written Japanese. Hikaru relearned the language he had been born into. As soon as he was ready, Hikaru booked passage back to Earth.

When He disembarked at the Tokyo Spaceport, absorbing the sights of the city which spread out before him, he revelled in an ecstasy of personal triumph. He had finally arrived at his Emerald City. "I felt like a weary traveller come home to new delights and admiration at my family's bravery. What a surprise awaited me!" said Sulu.

Hikaru took a cab to his dorm at the University, and set about unpacking. "I met my roommate, and prepared to introduce myself in Japanese. I got it out perfectly. Then my roommate laughed, saying, 'You speak like my grandfather.' That was my first shock. I already felt out of place in the one place I was sure I belonged," said Sulu.

And that's how it went for him. He was constantly out of step with contemporary Japanese culture, unable to get in sync. "When I went to Earth, I had visions of medievalism, samurai tradition, a place where I could step into a role and be accepted unconditionally. Instead of mountains and rolling hills, I saw a technopolis. I found out that, like on any of the other worlds I had visited, I still had to prove myself. In some ways, it was really worse. My relatives were disapproving of my family's lifestyle and treated me, well, not badly, but like a retarded stepchild. In the six months I ended up staying there, I found it no better or worse than any other planet," said Sulu of his first return to Earth since childhood.

Dejected and disillusioned, Sulu still had a keen desire to make a permanent home for himself somewhere where he would be accepted by his peers. Starfleet seemed an obvious second choice. Sulu was used to space travel and liked the diversity. Besides, he was beginning to wonder if he was destined to be planetbound. Sulu's next project was getting into the Academy. Wanting to attend and actually getting in were two very different things! He learned of the procedures and took the required achievement and aptitude tests. Much to his surprise, he found that while his achievement in applied mathematics was barely average, his aptitude was off the charts.

Sulu entered Starfleet Academy in the sciences section as a botany major. He did well in his classes, in spite of catch-up work in the theory of mathematics. Soon, he looked for something to fill his few spare hours. He found other fencers at the Academy and further developed his skills, building a powerful physique. Through enthusiasm and natural swashbuckling charm Sulu easily acquired friends and acquaintances. He found that he was a natural teacher; explaining things to others came easily. Sulu found people who appreciated his talents as well as his personality. He was finally making a place for himself.

He found that his tutoring abilities turned him into something of a "jack of all trades". In return for his help with some of the more mundane realities of Academy life, people showed him the more exciting things in life. One day, in return for emergency biochemistry lessons, a friend got Sulu onto the Academy helm trainers. Hikaru found himself fascinated. He experimented with the Academy's helm simulators, playing the same games he played with the ag station's hovercraft in his teen years.

He broke all sorts of simulator records, but while his instincts were excellent, his skill in mathematics was sadly lacking. Determined to rectify his deficiency, Sulu went to a friend. T'Skala was an engineering major, and one of her principle interests was helm and navigation design. With her help, Sulu's learned. T'Skala also showed his simulator tapes to her instructors. Realizing talent when they saw it, a professor quickly contacted Sulu and offered to change his field of study.

Sulu transfered his major to helm/navigation. After spending a childhood bouncing from one planet to the next with no control over his destination, piloting finally gave him a feeling of control over his own direction. He found that piloting ships brought real-life applicability to the mathematics he had difficulty with in high school.

His parents finally journeyed back to Earth to see their son graduate from the Academy and board the *USS Artemis* for his cadet cruise. The *Artemis* was a small scout that made runs between the Sol system and Alpha Centauri. As an assistant helm officer, Sulu enjoyed piloting the ship because of her small size. She responded quickly and sensitively under his deft hands.

After a year in space, Sulu returned to Earth a full commissioned ensign. He enlisted in Starfleet Academy Command School, Starfleet's "grad school" for those officers who want to gain their own commands. He attended Command School for a year, taking classroom sessions and simulations, including the fateful *Kobayashi Maru* no-win scenario.

In the simulation, the Klingons destroyed Sulu's ship piece by piece. When he realized his hopeless situation early on, he ordered his crew away in the life-pods, staying himself. He took the helm of the dying ship, and worked the same magic he did in the simulators, maniacally bent on trying to take as many Klingon warships as he could with him as an honor guard. Sulu did a respectable job; by the time his vessel blew into a million pieces, he had destroyed six Klingon cruisers, earning the all-time record.

Sulu graduated from Command School with an ability to command as well as a promotion to lieutenant, junior grade. With a distinguished record at the Academy, Starfleet posted Sulu to the destroyer *Xerxes* as a full helmsman. It was on the *Xerxes* that Sulu finally returned to deep space. While other young crewmembers were awestruck by deep space, Sulu felt a warm feeling inside. He was comfortable returning home.

Sulu continued to distinguish himself with exemplary piloting, most notably during the annual Starfleet Strategical Competition, a yearly Starfleet-wide "wargame"-type contest. Sulu finally brought the *Xerxes* home after a three-year mission in previously unexplored space.

His commander on the *Xerxes* saw something special in the young helmsman, and knew the new heavy cruisers would benefit by Sulu's superb piloting skill. The next one to be launched, the *Enterprise*, would need a helmsman of Sulu's talent, youthful tenacity, and enthusiasm.

George was born in the Boyle Heights district of Los Angeles and lived there until World War Two when his family was forcibly relocated to Arkansas by the United States government. From there they were moved again to another U.S. internment camp at Tule Lake in Northern California. The Takeis lived in one of the government run detention camp for Japanese Americans set up in the western United States during the final years of the World War Two. Although he now resents what was done, he was too young at the time to really understand what was happening to him.

George began his college education as an architecture student at the University of California at Berkeley. He later transferred to the Los Angeles Campus of the university, majoring in Theatre Arts with a minor in Latin American Studies. He graduated with a Bachelor of Arts degree in 1960.

While a student at U.C.L.A., George made his professional debut in a **Playhouse 90** production. Concurrent with his studies he furthered his training as an actor at the Desilu Workshop. George graduated with a Master's Degree in Theatre.

In 1962, George travelled to New York for what he describes as "the time honored actor's ritual of existence in cold water flats, off Broadway plays, odd jobs, an occasional live TV appearance, but mostly stark, unadulterated experience."

The following year brought major changes; he went to Europe. During his travels across the continent by bicycle, hitch-hiking and second-class trains, he sandwiched in attendance at the Shakespeare Institute at Stratford-on-Avon.

George's wanderlust took him back to America for camping expeditions into the rugged Rocky Mountains, a foray into the Alaskan panhandle, and numerous trips to Baja California.

When George returned to Hollywood, he found more leisure time than he liked despite his most energetic efforts to find acting work. He returned to U.C.L.A., garnering his Master's Degree in Theatre in 1964.

During that time, George racked up credits on such TV shows as **Perry Mason, Hawaiian Eye, The Islanders, Alcoa Premiere, Checkmate, Mr. Novak, The Wackiest Ship in the Army, I-Spy, The John Forsythe Show.** Over the years other appearances have been for such series as **Baa Baa Black Sheep, Bob Hope Chrysler Theatre, Bracken's World, Chico and the Man, Felony Squad, Ironside, It Takes a Thief, Kung Fu, Mr. Roberts, My Three Sons, The Six Million Dollar Man, Voyage to the Bottom of the Sea, The Twilight Zone** and many others.

During the first season of **Star Trek** he also worked in an appearance on **Mission: Impossible.**

George's feature film debut was in the movie **Ice Palace,** in which he co-starred with Richard Burton. George played a character who passed on-screen through the many years of his life. This required special aging makeup not un-

THE ACTOR

like that used in the **Star Trek** episode "The Deadly Years." His role in **Ice Palace** is both interesting and surprising, as he plays a stereotyped Japanese houseboy. It's incredible to be watching it and to suddenly realize that it's George Takei because the character is portrayed perfectly. It is like watching someone you know doing an imitation; quite funny.

George Takei's other motion picture credits include **A Majority of One, Red Line 7000, Hell to Eternity, An American Dream, Walk Don't Run, The Green Berets, Never So Few, Josie's Castle, The Loudmouth, The Young Divorcees PT 109** and **Which Way to the Front**.

George's interests extend well beyond acting, though. A political activist, he was elected to serve as a California delegate to the 1972 Democratic National Convention. In the fall of 1973, he ran unsuccessfully for Mayor Bradley's vacated council seat in Los Angeles, competing against twenty-two other candidates. During this campaign the local television station stopped showing Star Trek episodes featuring George because the other candidates threatened to demand equal time. When the final ballots were cast, George came in second.

Besides recreating the voice of Lt. Sulu on the Star Trek animated series, he's also appeared in all five motion pictures. Between the cancellation of Star Trek as a television show and the revival of the series as motion pictures, George continued to make occasional television appearances, including a dual role on an episode of **Hawaii Five-O**. He starred in a PBS production of the play "Year of the Dragon" in 1975 on **Theatre in America** for which he played a bitter Japanese American who hated his life as a tourist guide in L.A.'s "Little Tokyo." In the Eighties he played a drug lord on an episode of **Miami Vice**.

George also hosted an informational television series titled **Expression East/West** which dealt with issues involving human relationships. With author Robert Asprin, George co-wrote the science fiction novel *Mirror Friend, Mirror Foe* for the short-lived Playboy Press. A sequel has been discussed for some time.

George Takei is an individual who wears many different hats. He is a vowed lover of architecture, an actor, a writer and has been on the board of directors of the RTD (Southern California's Rapid Transit District) for ten years. As David Gerrold once put it, "he radiates energy". His enthusiasm shows in his work, whatever type it may be. In addition, he is one of the friendliest people you could meet. He loves meeting new people and getting embroiled in interesting conversations.

Our conversation soon turned to **Star Trek** and his reaction to the films.

"The first film was very interesting because it dealt with the relationship of man to machine or technology and defined that relationship as creator to created or lover to desired object. This runs all throughout the first film," Takei observed.

"When we first see Admiral Kirk, he is heading off to his only true mistress, the Enterprise, and Bill Shatner's face just captured such rapturous joy that you knew there was an incredible emotional achievement between this man and this machine. This is accentuated by the way the camera lovingly explores the soft curves of the ship, like a man gazing lovingly at his beloved just laying in repose before him.

"This is later picked up in the part of the story between Decker and Ilia-probe. Decker has this sexual feeling for a machine. In addition, we have the Enterprise itself penetrating V'Ger and exploring these pulsating, rounded orifices. I don't mean to get graphic here, but the film is filled with subtle sexual imagery.

"Finally at the end, the climax shall we say, we have this explosion of swirling light as a man and machine merge to form a new being that is compared to a baby. Gene Roddenberry added these subtexts to the film, which I found fascinating."

Takei notes that many fans had found the first film disappointing, perhaps because of its preponderance of admittedly beautiful special effects. "The second **Star Trek** film was more in keeping with the action and adventure spirit of the old series." He also compares the two directors. Robert Wise, he feels, was working under terrific deadline pressures but nonetheless was very meticulous and very prepared for each scene. He knew just what he wanted and he got it. Nicholas Meyer, George feels, was more of an improvising individual. He was also quite a character. "Now, Nick isn't very tall and he smokes this enormous cigar which he has with him everywhere he goes. It's like you see the end of this cigar and know that Nick will shortly be following after it. He liked to do Groucho Marx jokes with it and sometimes he would break into a beautiful Shakespearean soliloquy. He did a good job encouraging the actors to perform." Takei almost wasn't in **Star Trek II**. "When I first got the script and saw the kind of participation Sulu had, I saw that he wasn't much more than a talking prop. There was no character there, and I decided that I just couldn't go back under those conditions. My heart just wouldn't be in it. I told this to Harve Bennett and Nick Meyer, and they understood, but the script was al-

INTERVIEW

ready written and there wasn't much that they could do with it at that point. Anyway, I had to bow out at that point.

"Then came the first script rehearsal at Meyer's house. Everybody else was there except for Leonard (Nimoy) who was still back east filming **Marco Polo**. Nichelle Nichols looked around and noted that I wasn't there and asked, 'Where's George?' Well Nick explained and Bill (Shatner) said, 'All right, I'll handle this.' So Bill called me up at home and asked me why I wasn't there. I explained to him and told him that my heart was with them, but I just couldn't do the script under those conditions. Then he started pleading: 'We want you, George. We need you, George. We love you, George.' This was making it very hard for me because these people are my friends and I love them dearly, but I still said no. Bill said, 'Wait a minute, let me put Nichelle on.' Then came on this sexy voice and it said, 'We want you George. We need you, George. We love you, George.' Well that's hard to resist. So I said I'd talk with my agent and see what we could do.

"Anyway, Harve understood the problems and had a few scenes added that bolstered my part a little, but I was still unhappy. Filming was due to begin soon, and a decision had to be made. So they made me certain promises and I was on the set the first day of filming without even a contract. The first shots included me on the simulation bridge, so I was locked in.

"Unfortunately, when the film came out, some of the little scenes which would have added to my character ended up on the cutting room floor. Leonard knew how I felt, and so I had a much better part in the next film."

Takei has strong recollections of his experiences on **Star Trek II**. "Well," he says, "I remember Ike Eisenmann, who played Scotty's nephew, in make-up. You see, his first scene was the scene where Scotty comes on the bridge and he was dead already. He came early in the morning into make-up because there was an elaborate make-up job involved, and so by the time we came on the set, which was 7:00 or 7:30, he was pretty much in his make-up. He was shirtless from here (indicating his waist) on up, and the make-up covered his body as well as his face.

"There was a burned, shriveled, glistening glob of flesh hanging down from him, and he hopped out of his make-up chair and said, 'Morning, I'm Ike!' introducing himself with this flesh trembling on his side and blood oozing and some kind of bloody fluid just dripping off the side. Ugh. It was on the grotesque side. We would shake hands gingerly with him and then move away. We knew he was an actor in make-up, but it was such a grotesque sight that we couldn't go near him.

"He was a friendly guy and wanted to stand around and chat with us by the morning coffee urn area. We kept our distance and after a while he got the message. The poor kid. The first day he kept his distance from us out of consideration for our sensibilities.

"The costumes seem to have been changing from feature film to feature film," Takei states, "but **Star Trek III** was the first time when we didn't have that kind of uniform costume change. However, a good portion of this story took place when we change into our civilian clothes, so you got to see us in a lot of new costumes nevertheless. One of the things that I had some fun with was a leather cape. Of course, you know that Sulu fancies himself a swashbuckler of the 17th or 18th century, so he has good fun wearing his cape a lot of different ways.

"That made life and the job for my dresser awfully difficult because he has to keep track of how I wore it in each scene so that it matches any subsequent scene or preceding scene. He started by taking notes, but because I tried to be very creative in the way I used the cape, he was reduced to having a photographer there to take a shot of me each time the scene ended.

"Sulu does get to do a bit more in **Star Trek III** than he did in **Star Trek II**. He gets to demonstrate a good deal of his martial arts prowess and he gets into this complication with a seven foot tall, blonde Viking!" Takei praises Leonard Nimoy's direction of the film and has a high regard for his dedication to the project.

"There is one very elaborate scene set on this futuristic world which uses all these gorgeous costumes. Bob Fletcher, who is the costume designer on the film, found these exquisite bolts of silk and cloth down in a cellar that Cecil B. DeMille had bought years ago and which had been forgotten. He had a field day coming up with these gorgeous designs. They were so good that I would have volunteered to wear one had I not already been involved.

"Now Paramount didn't want to spend the money on this expensive scene. They felt that it could be described in a few lines of dialogue and thus save them a lot of money. Leonard felt that he owed the public this scene and he fought for it by pounding on a few desks and in the end, they gave it to him. I must say that they got their money's worth; every cent shows up there on the screen. By the end of the film, everyone was very happy with Leonard. He had managed to bring the film in under time and under budget, which is quite a feat for a first time director of a feature film."

As a child, Takei lived in World War II Japanese-American internment camps in Arkansas and Northern California. He says that, "I must confess, the guard towers and barbed-wire (in a film he acted in where he portrays a Japanese prisoner of war) brought back boyhood memories. But then, as a child, those surroundings seemed natural to me. I didn't really understand what they meant, or the anguish my parents went through until I was older."

Although approved by Congress, reparations of $20,000 to each surviving Japanese-American internee are yet to be disbursed. Takei, who's been an outspoken supporter of the payments, plans to donate his to the Japanese-American National Museum currently under construction in Little Tokyo in Los Angeles. "But I don't care if I have to wait," he says. "What's critically important is that those who were hurt the worst, who are senior citizens now, receive redress as quickly as possible. It's already too late for my father. He passed away in 1979."

George Takei continues to stand for a better future, both on and off screen.

THE
NAVIGATOR

Pavel Chekov, the only child of Ivan and Paulina Chekov, was born in the Russian city of Leningrad. Ivan, the elected manager of the city, was driven hard by his work, and at an early age insisted his son go through advanced schooling to make his motherland proud. Ivan would take his son on his knee and tell him larger-than-life stories about the heroes of old Mother Russia. For Ivan, Earth was built on Russian culture and technology.

Paulina also wanted her son to succeed, but she encouraged him to make friends and enjoy life. Even in school, much more was expected of Pavel than of other boys. After all, he was the son of a city manager who had nothing in his youth and achieved power through perseverance. Ivan was a popular leader, who worked hard for what he got, and Pavel was expected to achieve twice what his father did.

Pavel did have friends, but they too were the "gifted children" of whom great things were expected. Even when Pavel went out after school with his friends, their work was discussed constantly. Paulina convinced the men in her family to acquiesce and take vacations, but wherever they went, Paulina would end up relaxing while her husband made personal political contacts and her son studied the local history.

Pavel had adjusted to this intensity. During holiday breaks from school, young Pavel became bored. He would do even more advanced work and pull further ahead of his peers.

Pavel's one weak spot was a girl named Irina Galilulan. She was beautiful, and fiercely intelligent. Pavel had mixed feelings for her. She was his primary academic rival, yet there was something about her. When he was with her, he felt free of his duty to excel in his studies. What he felt was warm and consuming, completely exhilarating.

It was amusing that every other sentence out of Pavel's mouth was "Irina and I did this today," or "Irina is doing well today," or a hundred variations. Pavel had never spoken of his friends this way before. Paulina could see her son falling in love, even if he didn't know it or dare admit it if he did. Pavel was beginning his teen years, his adolescence.

Paulina had been an exchange student on Vulcan many years before, and while she respected their drive for success and their system of logic, she had married a human. It turned out he might as well have been a Vulcan but for pointed ears. She didn't want her son to fall into the same trap. Non-emotion was very good for Vulcans, but humans needed their emotions. Human society was based on emotion, and Paulina didn't want her son to miss out on anything that was human.

Paulina would stay out in the afternoons so Irina and Pavel could visit privately. Pavel's father, Ivan, wasn't too keen on the idea. At first he considered his son's interest in Irina to be a healthy, but fleeting, teenage phase, but as Pavel became more serious with Irina over months and then years, he began to put

PROFILE

his foot down. He said, "Do as I did son: gain success, then worry about finding a good woman."

As a result, Pavel was torn in several directions. His father wanted him to be more serious-minded, his mother wanted him to know the joys of romance and love. Irina was becoming more and more discontented with her strict rigorous program of studies. She was telling Pavel about a different life, a freer life concentrating much more on needs of the human spirit than on the needs of human society. Pavel wanted to do his duty, make his father proud, enjoy the sweet romance of the moment and share it with his mother, and he wanted to love Irina and spend his life with her.

Frequently after school, Irina took Pavel to a wilderness area a distance from the city. Pavel had been there before, to collect biological data for analysis. This was different for Pavel, alone with the woman he loved. The trees were greener, the sounds of the birds and the insects louder. There was warmth in her hand in his as she showed Pavel to be free to live with nature. She showed him how to build a shelter, which flora were edible, how to follow the creatures of nature in silence so as to see their total uninhibited beauty.

Irina pressured Pavel into forgetting his exacting, meticulous, demanding studies, to join her in her "escape" to a less structured life. Pavel was tempted. He was honestly tempted by the chance to do what Pavel Chekov wanted to do; not what Ivan wanted him to do; not what society dictated he should do; but what Pavel Chekov wanted to do. Each night in the Chekov household, Ivan would bring home more opportunities to his son for his future if only his son remain diligent in his studies as he had been in the past. Pavel couldn't bear to let his father down and waste all of the opportunities his father had been working to get for him.

Irina finally forced her lover to choose between the freedom she offered and the security and opportunity held out by his father. She had had enough of what she thought was needless self-denial in the name of a "duty" that was nothing more than bureaucratic flag-waving and drum-beating. She was leaving to join her friends in the city; leaving to find their own corner of nature to live the way they wanted. Irina pleaded with Pavel to join her, spoke of beaches to walk on, children to share and life to enjoy together. Pavel reminded her of her studies, the investment she, her parents, and society had made into her skills. He told her she had to do what was right and honor her parents, live up to society's expectations.

She rejected that outright, saying her life was her own to live. Pavel told her of the grand opportunities that lie before them if only they persevered. She told him he was unfeeling; she wanted him to leave.

That was the last time for years Pavel would see Irina. The following day she was not in school, and after school Pavel couldn't find her at her house. Her parents told him she had disappeared completely, without a note. Pavel frantically searched the city for any trace of Irina. He searched the wilderness that they had

played in. No one had seen her. Pavel figured she had gone looking for her little piece of nature.

For many months Pavel was despondent. Irina had been there for so long, now without her there was a hole in his life. His father kept pushing him, telling him that life would go on; Irina wasn't important to Pavel's future.

Pavel graduated from high school with honors, and several universities in Pavel's home country made very appealing offers. But for Pavel Leningrad had grown stark, empty, bleak and hollow. Without Irina there was nothing for him. Distance had grown between Pavel and his parents, a distance never bridged except by Irina.

Upon his graduation, Starfleet Academy invited Pavel to apply. At first Pavel ignored that option as frivolous; he had no time to play at adventure. Yet there was no enthusiasm to attend any other university. Pavel finally decided to apply to the Academy — to get away from Leningrad, even if for only a short time. His mother was concerned for her son's safety in Starfleet; his father for the first moment in a very long time, supportive of his son's choice. His father expected Starfleet to be respectable temporary steppingstone for Pavel; Ivan himself had served honorably in the Merchant Marine for a brief time. It had taught good discipline.

Although Starfleet's tests proved rough, Pavel had been accustomed to the difficult, and he scored exceptionally high. Pavel found Starfleet as rigorous as his earlier advanced intensive classes. The attitude behind the hard work was different at the Academy, though. Pavel's father had always pushed discipline as "patriotism," obligation; in Starfleet cadets accepted self-discipline because they craved it. The cadets felt purpose behind the hard work, goals they wanted to attain. Pavel Chekov came to respect this voluntary self-imposed rigor more than the forced control of his youth. To Pavel, giving of yourself because you wanted to meant more than obligatory sacrifice.

Upon graduation from the Academy with the highest achievement honors, Pavel was assigned to the *USS Hannibal*, a destroyer, as his cadet cruise. As an assistant navigator, Pavel manned the usually quiet overnight graveyard shift. The *Hannibal* was frequently assigned to the Klingon border, and became involved several border dispute skirmishes, always repelling the Klingon invaders. Pavel was always on top of things for his captain, yet never proceeded without authorization. The captain of the *Hannibal* began to take notice of this young crewman, of his readiness to serve and his levelheadedness in battle while others around him were losing their head. The *Hannibal*'s commander noted Pavel was more skilled at the navigation console than were many veterans. The skipper commended the young officer, and promoted him to assistant chief navigator.

After the year's cadet mission was over, Pavel returned to Starfleet Academy to attend the year-long Command School, in which he again distinguished himself. Pavel performed exactingly and methodically during the entire *Kobayashi Maru* test; everything was done in safety and by the book. While Pavel and his ship went down at the hands of the computer-driven Klingon fleet, his decisiveness saved more of the lives of his crew than did most other cadets. Pavel dreamed of the day he could command a starship of his own.

Now an ensign, Starfleet posted Pavel aboard his first deep space five year mission, aboard the heavy cruiser *Enterprise*. Her commander, James T. Kirk, was looking for exactly what Pavel Chekov had to offer: skill, a cool head and efficiency. Ensign Chekov would learn quite a bit about command from Kirk, making Kirk his mentor. Kirk was efficient, possessed of a cool head, but also flexible enough to encompass all needs. He contained relaxed reassurance in the competency of his crew, making each one feel important. Pavel Chekov hoped to one day master a starship as well as his captain.

Walter Koenig was born in Chicago but grew up in the Inwood area of Manhattan where he attended grade school. He graduated from the Fieldston High School of the Ethical Culture School System in Riverdale, New York and made his stage debut playing the title role in a production of "Peer Gynt." He also appeared in "The Devil's Disciple."

During the summer months he worked with underprivileged children in camps in upstate New York. There he instituted a theatre program which was, in truth, a thinly disguised psychodrama for disturbed and overly aggressive youngsters. This program was later incorporated into the camp's parent settlement house where, to his knowledge, it is still in existence.

Koenig spent his first two years of college as a pre-med student at Grinell College in Iowa, with the intention of becoming a psychiatrist, and performed in summer stock in Vermont during his vacation.

He relocated to the West Coast with his mother and brother following the death of his father. He completed his education at U.C.L.A., graduating with a B.A. in Psychology.

Following graduation Koenig returned to New York and was enrolled at the Neighborhood Playhouse upon the recommendation of Prof. Friedman, with whom he had studied at U.C.L.A. To meet expenses during this period, he worked as a hospital orderly, earning $75 a month. After another two years of doing off-Broadway work, Koenig returned to Los Angeles to play a variety of stage and television roles.

On television he's appeared as a Swedish businessman, an American grape-picker, an Arabian rock and roll singer and a French resistance fighter. His television credits include appearances on **Mr. Novak, The Great Adventure, Gidget, Jerrico, The Lieutenant, Ben Casey, Combat, Ironside, Mannix, Medical Center, The Men from Shiloh, The Untouchables, I-Spy, The Questor Tapes** and two appearances on **The Starlost** in the role of the alien, Oro. He also had a prominent role in a one-hour episode of **Alfred Hitchcock Presents** in the early Sixties titled "Memo From Purgatory" which was written by Harlan Ellison. In films he appeared in the movie **Deadly Honeymoon** as well as in all five **Star Trek** motion pictures.

On stage Koenig played three roles in the highly acclaimed theatre group production of "The Deputy;" that of a Jewish refugee, a Nazi sergeant and a Catholic monk. He also played a Welsh psychopath in "Night Must Fall."

Koenig has extended his talents into the area of writing as well and wrote the episode "The Infinite Vulcan" for the animated **Star Trek** and the episode "The Stranger" for **Land of the Lost.** He's also written scripts for such television series as **Class of '65** and **Family.** In the book field he wrote a behind-the-scenes log about his experiences making **Star Trek: The Motion Picture** called *Chekov's Enterprise.* In 1988 he had a science fiction novel published called *Buck Alice and the Actor Robot.*

THE ACTOR

As the character Ensign Chekov, Koenig didn't join the **Star Trek** TV cast until the second season. At the time it was reported this was done because of a complaint in the Soviet newspaper *Pravda* regarding the absence of Russians aboard the *Enterprise*, but Koenig later revealed that this as a pure publicity stunt. During the second season, Chekov was not an established regular, but gained a more secure status on the series when George Takei took a ten week leave of absence to appear in **The Green Berets** with John Wayne and Sulu was thus missing from the ship.

Probably Koenig's best role on the series was in the episode "Mirror, Mirror" in which Koenig played the sly, ruthless alternate universe Chekov who nearly succeeds in assassinating Captain Kirk.

Koenig continued to act following the cancellation of the **Star Trek** TV series in 1969. Prior to the revival of **Star Trek** as a film series, he performed occasional television roles such as one for an episode of **Columbo** as well as in the tele-movie **The Questor Tapes**.

Koenig regained back the rights to *Chekov's Enterprise* and is planning to have a new edition of the book published.

In September, 1989, Walter Koenig and his wife, Judy, appeared on the Los Angeles radio show "Hour 25" delivering a dramatic reading of an unproduced **Twilight Zone** script titled "Say Hello, Mr. Quigley."

By Mary Sue Uram

Walter Koenig, **Star Trek**'s Russian navigator Chekov, explains what it is like being directed by fellow actor Leonard Nimoy, "Terrific. It was a wonderful experience. He's very sensitive, very well prepared and he really cared about the actors. He dealt with us all on an individual basis. I had no way of knowing this because playing the part of the character (Spock), he's rather distant and aloof. But when he dropped that character, he became very human, very close, a warm person. It was really neat working with him. I think we all felt that way.

"He did as much as he could with what was offered within the parameters of the script. He can't change the script."

Gene Roddenberry was the father of **Star Trek** and yet he is little involved with the series of movies. Koenig notes that, "We miss him as the creator of the show. There has to be a certain affection for the man who joined us all originally. I think we've all made friends with him. Most of us were friends to begin with.

"We're a good family. We've always gotten along very well, and I think we pull for each other. I really do. I know that there would be some scene in **Star Trek** where the very first people who came up to me were George (Takei), Jimmy (Doohan), DeForest (Kelley) and Nichelle (Nichols), that said it worked well. I felt the same for them."

Koenig says his part in **Star Trek III** was "very small. However, I am resigned to that with good nature thus far. I needed to have a broader view and I see that it's only fair that the other people, the other supporting actors, get more to do. I had a better part among the supporting people in **Star Trek II**, and to be sure, George has some really cute things. He does some martial arts in **Star Trek III**. Nichelle has a scene where she vamps a young Lieutenant. Jimmy's dialogue is very funny. I think Nichelle has the funniest line in the film. I think they are all shown to good advantage.

"I wasn't that impressed on reading the script, mainly because I wasn't impressed with the character (Chekov), the way the character was written. And it did, to a considerable degree, color my reaction. I am, after all, only human and capable of human foible and weakness and all that pettiness that everybody else is. And it probably did have an effect on my reaction."

Koenig did enjoy better moments in the fourth **Star Trek** film, although perhaps not in the fifth.

INTERVIEW

THE
NURSE

The humanoid known to the universe as Christine Chapel was "born" on Larmia VI, a Federation member who produced its offspring through genetic engineered efforts without a "mother" or "father." Reproductive cells are taken from various Larmian male and female volunteers and sent to Offspring Centers where technicians experiment with these fertilized cells to obtain the best possible results. A cell is first kept in a growth solution in small monitored containers, but as the fetus develops, it is moved into larger and larger incubators. Each year this process yields exactly 200 male and female young.

These children are designated and ranked based on their comparison to their "siblings." Many Federation races found this system cold and unfeeling towards children, but the Larmians explain that, contrary to other genetic experiments, Larmian children who don't make top standards are not murdered but instead treated with the same respect as the top ten percent "harvested" that year.

The being who would later call herself Chapel was assessed at a rank of twenty-seventh out of 200, and that year's lot number was attached. She was commonly referred to as Number Twenty-Seven. Chapel looked almost identical to her "sister," known as Number One. Both had been contrived from reproductive cells from the same elder Larmian volunteer. Number Twenty-Seven and Number One became friends, but were separated much of the time because of Number One's super-intensive training, required of the top ten children each year.

Although Number Twenty-Seven was still quite an accomplished rank, her genetic engineering wasn't as "perfect" as those ranked above her. Number Twenty-Seven was both physically and mentally superb, but her emotions weren't as controlled as those of Number One. As much as emotional state can be controlled by genetics, Number One was made as stable as possible.

Unlike Vulcans, the Larmians were not unemotional. The Larmians looked upon forgetting emotion as not taking advantage of an asset, a tool. Emotions, to the Larmians, made people complete. The Larmians, however, stressed controlled, appropriate emotional responses. Each shade of emotion — from glee to red hate — , for the Larmians, was appropriate for certain situations. Appropriateness is what they try to impress on their young.

Number Twenty Seven's schooling — like that of every other young Larmian — was broken into two parts, an indoctrination in facts and social training. Fact-learning was done in a dream state. Young Larmians were made open to dreams that illustrated learning situations. Number Twenty-Seven was instructed in her dreams. One dream would consist of memorizing and analyzing algebra equations; another would consist of a chemistry experiment. This went on for ten years after they reached their fifth or sixth birthday.

The second part of Number Twenty-Seven's education was "social training." She and other Larmian children spent their days experimenting in various real-life social situations in which they discovered appropriate mental and emotional responses. Larmian children spent their everyday lives pretty much free to

PROFILE

get themselves in all sorts of situations. The children would steal others' property and have it stolen from them, all under the guidance of their elders. Then the children would analyze the situation, and with the advice of their elders, formulate an understanding that stealing was wrong, and that there were appropriate actions to take if their belongings were stolen from them. Millions of different scenarios taught Larmian children everything from the answers to large moral questions to such small everyday matters as sharing a common bathroom. And this is what Number Twenty-Seven experienced during her ten years of education growing up on Larmia VI.

"Many offworlders conceptualize Larmia as a boring place because all this is planned," Number Twenty-Seven later said after she joined Starfleet and became Nurse Christine Chapel. "It isn't boring in the way they think. Larmia has business and art and it can all be dramatic. Fierce competition is only natural in a society in which the government ranks you. If you can change your ranking, great. The government considers competition 'appropriate' because it's a tool of development. So many different things can happen on Larmia. Passion and excitement are considered appropriate by the government, so Larmia has some wonderful art and literature, but violence and crime aren't considered 'appropriate,' so Larmia is very safe.

"I left Larmia because of the way it limited me. After a while, I was tired of 'appropriate.' I longed for spontaneity, randomness. Until I was much older, probably until I got on the *Enterprise* and Mr. Spock was going through pon farr, I had never gotten yelled at for an 'inappropriate' reason. It was both exciting and scary.

"Also, because my genetic make-up wasn't as good as Number One's, I was more prone to inappropriate emotion. She was good command material, which called for a person to be appropriate and somewhat obsessive. Number One was like that, she'd fixate on problems until she would work them out. Starfleet was her first choice, because she enjoyed solving problems on a large scale, which is what command in Starfleet is all about.

"I entered the Starfleet Nursing School because I had emotions for taking care of people that weren't always welcome on Larmia, and also because I was curious. Like I said, I wanted to get a little chaotic, and most of the galaxy is pretty chaotic.

"I changed my name because I thought it was more personal. I always wanted to be truly close to people, maybe that closeness was hard to achieve on Larmia. Christine Chapel sounded warm, flowing, and comfortable. I hoped it would soothe my patients more than 'Twenty-Seven' would. Number One never had to change her name because it described her perfectly, because it gave her that air of authority she wanted," Christine explained.

Christine did well in nursing school on Earth, enjoying her interaction with the patients, feeling truly needed. Upon graduation, Starfleet put her on the *USS Exeter*, a deep-space mission, as a staff nurse. Her superior was chief medical officer, Dr. Roger Korby. He was a brilliant physician and researcher, diving into the medical technology of every new culture the *Exeter* discovered, adding new knowledge to the Federation.

At first she admired and respected him, then she fell in love with him for his dedication and the passion in him that produced that dedication. Korby was a man with presence; he commanded attention. He was dedicated and determined, alive with fire. Christine was attracted to the raw emotion that was so new to her. At first Korby refused to get involved with a subordinate, but when they got to know each other better, Korby realized that under her Larmian t raining, she was a sensual woman possessed of great passion, and he could no longer resist.

They soon became engaged, but just a few months later Korby was reported missing-in-action from a first contact landing party while investigating an ancient culture in which the androids were slowly taking over. The *Exeter* remained in orbit for days in a desperate search that proved fruitless. Eventually, sadly, the *Exeter*'s commander declared the incident closed and the starship moved on. Christine cried for days. She found then, as well as later on, that she was overcome by raging extremes of emotion that she had never experienced before. Although she tried very hard, the chaotic emotions proved beyond her control.

After Korby was lost, Christine returned to Earth to finish her lost fiancee's research. Within four months, she had pulled herself back together, thanks largely to her "sister" in Starfleet, Number One, who was already captain of her own destroyer, the *El Cid*. Number One's somber reasoning reassured Christine that she was still sane and that life must go on.

Christine transfered aboard the *Enterprise* as Chief Nurse for her five year deep space mission already in progress. Her new CMO was as dedicated as Korby but not as arrogantly passionate. Dr. Leonard McCoy was passionate in a down-to-earth, gentle way. She was, however, intrigued — and attracted to — the Vulcan first officer, Mr. Spock. Christine could sense the same raging fire of emotions beneath the surface that Roger had, only Spock's was cloaked in the mystique of his alien land.

Born Majel Lee Hudec, she grew up in Cleveland, Ohio and graduated from Shaker Heights High School. In Cleveland she majored in Theatre Arts at Flora Stone Mather College for Women, of Western Reserve University. Then Barrett transferred to the University of Miami where she majored in Theatre Arts. Following a year at law school, she relocated to New York City to pursue acting.

Barrett's initial work as an actress included eleven weeks of summer stock in Bermuda and a play, "Models By Season," staged in Boston. The play nearly made it to Broadway but closed out of town, as they say.

Following a nine month tour in the play "The Solid Gold Cadillac," she travelled to California to appear in the play "All for Mary" with Edward Everett Horton at the Pasadena Playhouse. While studying drama with Anthony Quinn, he was impressed with her talent to the degree that he helped her obtain work with Paramount Pictures. For Paramount, Barrett appeared in three films: **Black Orchid, As Young as We Are** and **The Buccaneer** which featured Quinn and was directed by the legendary Cecil B. DeMille. She then studied dramatic acting under Sanford Meisner, comedy under Lucille Ball, and was signed to a contract with Desilu, the studio then owned by Lucille Ball.

Prior to **Star Trek**, Barrett appeared on such shows as **77 Sunset Strip, I Love Lucy, Bonanza, Dr. Kildare, The Eleventh Hour, Here Come the Brides, The Lieutenant, Love on a Rooftop, Many Happy Returns, Pete and Gladys, Please Don't Eat the Daisies, The Second Hundred Years, Wackiest Ship in the Army, Westinghouse Playhouse** and **The Untouchables**. She also appeared as a regular for a time on **Leave it to Beaver** as Gwenn Rutherford, Lumpy's mother, from 1958 to '63.

Her other film credits include **Track of Thunder, The Domino Principle, Guide to the Married Man, Love in a Goldfish Bowl, The Quick and the Dead, Sylvia** and **Westworld**.

As Nurse Chapel, Majel Barrett remained with **Star Trek** from the beginning to the end. In fact, before the show was even accepted she had appeared in the first pilot as the coldly intelligent Number One, a role which she played quite convincingly and which was far more interesting than her minor role as Dr. McCoy's nurse. Barrett was also the voice of the computer on the **Star Trek** TV series, a role she is repeating for **Star Trek: The Next Generation**.

In the first **Star Trek** pilot, now telecast as part of "The Menagerie," she is billed as Lee Hudec, as Roddenberry had been told to get rid of "that character." But he wanted to use Majel in another role in the series. Majel became Mrs. Gene Roddenberry on August 6, 1969, following the cancellation of **Star Trek**, in a Buddhist-Shinto ceremony in Tokyo, Japan. They have a son who was born on February 5th, 1974, named Eugene Wesley Roddenberry, Jr.

Since **Star Trek** Barrett has appeared in Gene Roddenberry's pilots **Genesis II, Planet Earth, Spectre** and **The Questor Tapes**. She returned as *Doctor*

THE ACTOR

Chapel in **Star Trek: The Motion Picture**, but was then excluded from subsequent films until returning in **Star Trek IV: The Voyage Home**.

Barrett has appeared on two episodes of **Star Trek: The Next Generation** in a recurring role as the mother of Deana Troi, playing an overbearing and obnoxious telepath.

Barrett also runs Lincoln Enterprises, a mail order business dealing in **Star Trek** memorabilia and other film related merchandise such as scripts, posters and the like. Occasionally she appears at **Star Trek** conventions representing Lincoln and selling official merchandise.

Her off-screen hobbies include goldworking, gem cutting and gourmet cooking, as well as golfing.

When **Star Trek** was first put on film in the form of the pilot now referred to as "The Cage," Majel Barrett was there as part of the cast. Playing an unusual character known only as Number One, she was a senior officer on the *Enterprise* under Captain Christopher Pike. When NBC requested revisions and a second pilot, one of their directives was to get rid of this disturbing female character who was portrayed as being the equal of men. So Gene Roddenberry recast Barrett as a nurse in the new cast, gave her blond hair and the network was never the wiser. Barrett has continued her involvement with **Star Trek**, appearing in the first and the fourth motion pictures, as well as playing an entirely new character who has appeared in a couple episodes of **Star Trek: The Next Generation**.

Barrett, by being on board for the first version of **Star Trek**, was able to see how the show was being treated like a poor stepchild even before a foot of film had been shot. Instead of shooting on the Desilu lot, the cast and crew of "The Cage" were sent some miles away to Culver City to the old Goldwyn Studios. They had plenty of room there to set up because nothing else was shooting on that lot at the time. Due to the expense that would have been incurred by having Susan Oliver come in for make-up tests, Barrett stood in to test the green body paint slated to be used for the Orion slave girl.

Barrett relates the following story, "While this make-up was on, we were really remote from everything, and suddenly we were through with one of the tests and somebody yelled: Lunch! We looked around and there was nothing there. No restaurant. No commissary. Nothing. You had to walk out to the sidewalk, down the street and over to Washington Boulevard to go into a restaurant. And needless to say, Leonard (replete with experimental Vulcan ears) and I arm-in-armed it down the street. The cars honked, of course, the tooting, the stopping, the screeching and so forth. You expect that because even by Hollywood standards we looked strange.

"When we entered the restaurant, the waitress automatically did a double-take, and the cast went into hysterical fits of laughter. We tried to ignore it, but the entire place was looking at us all the time. It's hard to eat like that. You know when someone is watching you, and you know how silly you look and how silly you feel. And here Leonard was looking at this green monster of some sort sitting across from him, and I was looking at this pointy-eared goblin, who—when he chews his food—his ears wiggle. Needless to say, we brown-bagged it from then on."

Later, after the second pilot had been filmed and **Star Trek** had been picked up as a series, Barrett was back aboard as the nurse, only now the hijinks took place behind the scenes instead of on public streets.

"I remember John D.F. Black; the things we did to him were terrible. On his first day as story consultant on **Star Trek**, a new job, Gene said to him, 'Look, I've got this actress coming in. I really don't have time to see her, so just talk to her for me.' He said, 'Well, what do I say?' And George said, 'I don't know, just put her off somehow or other.' John sat there and they sent *me* up. Now, I was prepared with this white bikini-type bathing suit on, and I went in

INTERVIEW

and said, 'Mr. Black, I understand you are casting this movie and I really need.
. . ' and all this time I'm taking my clothes off. Now this was John's first day
on the job, and he sat there, his chair up against the second floor window—I
thought he was going to fall out! He started saying, 'No! No! I don't want it to
go this way!' Well everyone else was outside waiting for the proper moment to
come in—which had gone past. I was down to nothing, practically. They finally opened up the door and said, 'John! What are you doing?!' At this point—
the poor man—the telephone rings. It's his wife. She wants to know about his
first day at work. I don't know if he'll ever forgive me."

In 1979 Barrett returned as Dr. Chapel aboard the reconditioned *Enterprise* in
Star Trek: The Motion Picture in a part which gave her more to do than just
stand at Dr. McCoy's elbow. But beginning with the second **Star Trek** film,
Paramount restricted Gene Roddenberry's involvement and this was particularly expressed in excising Dr. Chapel from the cast. When asked about this while
Star Trek III was in production, Barrett replied, "Apparently Paramount
thinks that if one Roddenberry doesn't work, neither Roddenberry works."

By the time **Star Trek IV** was to be made, Paramount and the Roddenberrys
were on better terms. Dr. Chapel returned as a Lieutenant Commander working
in Starfleet Command Headquarters in San Francisco.

"It was marvelous being back on the set with everyone," she states enthusiasti-
cally. "I don't have much to do in the film, but it was nice being back in front
of the cameras and working." Barrett appears near the beginning and at the end
of the film, but not on the *Enterprise* this time. A scene she had filmed with
Mark Lenard was cut when it was decided that for dramatic purposes the character of Sarek would be introduced during the debate in the Starfleet council
chambers rather than talking with Chapel before entering the chambers to challenge the Klingon delegate.

During the first year of **Star Trek: The Next Generation**, Majel Barrett
turned up in two roles. One was as the familiar voice of the ship's computer
which she had done throughout the original **Star Trek** series in the Sixties and
which she copied exactly when doing the voice for the computer aboard the
new *Enterprise*. On-screen she was seen in the episode "Haven" as Lwaxana
Troi, the overbearing mother of ship's counselor Deanna Troi. She reprised the
character in the second season of **Star Trek: The Next Generation** as well,
but was not seen in **Star Trek V**.

"I don't see much of a future for Christine Chapel," Barrett stated in 1987 in a
magazine devoted to **The Next Generation**. "I really see much more of a future for Majel Barrett playing Lwaxana Troi. Lwaxana is sort of the Auntie
Mame of the galaxy. She's a much more fun character, and I can play her forever because I'm at an age where that's totally believable. I would like to continue to do that. I could leave Chapel very easily. However, if somebody gave
me the chance to do her again, of course I would."

James Van Hise created **Enterprise Incidents** over a decade ago. He has served as editor ever since. In addition, he also serves as editor and publisher of the highly successful **Midnight Graffiti,** and is author of such nonfiction books as *Batmania, How to Draw Art For Comic Books: Lessons From the Masters and Stephen King and Clive Barker: The Illustrated Masters of the Macabre.*

THE AUTHOR

The World's Only
Official
COUCH
POTATO
BOOK
CATALOG™

Please note:
You must be a certified couch potato* to partake of
this offering!

* To become a certified couch potato you must watch a minimum of 25 hours a
day at least 8 days per week.

From Happy Hal...

Star Trek
Gunsmoke
The Man from U.N.C.L.E.

They all evoke golden memories of lost days of decades past. What were you doing when you first saw them?

Were you sitting with your parents and brothers and sisters gathered around a small set in your living room?

Were you in your own apartment just setting out on the wonders of supporting yourself, with all of the many associated fears?

Or were you off at some golden summer camp with all of the associated memories, of course forgetting the plague of mosquitoes and the long, arduous hikes?

The memories of the television show are mixed with the memories of the time in a magical blend that always brings a smile to your face. Hopefully we can help bring some of the smiles to life, lighting up your eyes and heart with our work...

Look inside at the **UNCLE Technical Manual**, the **Star Trek Encyclopedia**, **The Compleat Lost in Space** or the many, many other books about your favorite television shows!

Let me know what you think of our books.

And what you want to see.

It's the only way we can share our love of the wonders of the magic box....

Selection

HAL SCHUSTER

Administration

JACK SCHUSTER,
COUCH POTATO

Customer Service

PHYLLIS SCHUSTER

From The Couch Potato...

I am here working hard on your orders.

Let me tell you about a few new things we have added to help speed up your order. First we are computerizing the way we process your order so that we can more easily look it up if we need to and maintain our customer list. The program will also help us process our shipping information by including weight, location and ordering information which will be essential if you have a question or complaint (Heavens Forbid).

We are now using UPS more than the post office. This helps in many ways including tracing a package if it is lost and in more speedily getting your package to you because they are quicker. . They are also more careful with shipments and they arrive in better condition. UPS costs a little more than post office, This is unfortunate but we feel you will find that it is worth it.

Also please note our new discount program. Discounts range from 5% to 20% off.

So things are looking up in 1988 for Coach Potato.

I really appreciate your orders and time but I really must get back to the tube...

THE COUCH POTATO BOOK CATALOG   5715 N BALSAM, LAS VEGAS, NV   89130

The Phantom
The Green Hornet
The Shadow
The Batman

Each issue of Serials Adventures Presents offers 100 or more pages of pure nostalgic fun for $16.95

SERIALS ADVENTURES MAGAZINE

Flash Gordon Part One
Flash Gordon Part Two
Blackhawk

Each issue of Serials Adventures Presents features a chapter by chapter review of a rare serial combined with biographies of the stars and behind-the-scenes information. Plus rare photos. See the videotapes and read the books!

UNCLE

THE U.N.C.L.E. TECHNICAL MANUAL

Every technical device completely detailed and blueprinted, including weapons, communications, weaponry, organization, facitilites... 80 pages. 2 volumes...$9.95 each

PRISONER

NUMBER SIX: THE COMPLEAT PRISONER

The most unique and intelligent television series ever aired! Patrick McGoohan's tour-de-force of spies and mental mazes finally explained episode by episode, including an interview with the McGoohan and the complete layout of the real village!...160 pages...$14.95

GREEN HORNET TELEVISION

THE GREEN HORNET

Daring action adventure with the Green Hornet and Kato. This show appeared before Bruce Lee had achieved popularity but delivered fun, superheroic action. Episode guide and character profiles combine to tell the whole story...120 pages...$14.95

WILD, WILD, WEST

WILD, WILD, WEST

Is it a Western or a Spy show? We couldn't decide so we're listing it twice. Fantastic adventure, convoluted plots, incredible devices...all set in the wild, wild west! Details of fantastic devices, character profiles and an episode-by-episode guide...120 pages...$17.95

THE COUCH POTATO BOOK CATALOG 5715 N BALSAM, LAS VEGAS, NV   89130

THE COUCH POTATO BOOK CATALOG 5715 N BALSAM, LAS VEGAS, NV 89130

TREK YEAR 1
The earliest voyages and the creation of the series. An in-depth episode guide, a look at the pilots, interviews, character profiles and more...
160 pages...$10.95

TREK YEAR 2
TREK YEAR 3
$12.95 each

THE ANIMATED TREK
Complete inone volume $14.95

THE MOVIES
The chronicle of all the movies...
116 pages...$12.95

THE LOST YEARS
For the first time anywhere, the exclusive story of the Star Trek series that almost was including a look at every proposed adventure and an interview with the man that would have replaced Spock. Based on interviews and exclusive research...
160 pages...$14.95

NEXT GENERATION
Complete background of the new series. Complete first season including character profiles and actor biographies...160 pages
...$19.95

THE TREK ENCYCLOPEDIA
The reference work to Star Trek including complete information on every character, alien race and monster that ever appeared as well as full information on every single person that ever worked on the series from the stars to the stunt doubles from extras to producers, directors, make-up men and cameramen...**over 360 pages. UPDATED EDITION. Now includes planets, ships and devices**...$19.95

INTERVIEWS ABOARD THE ENTERPRISE
Interviews with the cast and crew of Star Trek and the Next Generation. From Eddie Murphy to Leonard Nimoy and from Jonathan Frakes to Marina Sirtis. Over 100 pages of your favorites.
$18.95

THE ULTIMATE TREK
The most spectacular book we have ever offered. This volume completely covers every year of Star Trek, every animated episode and every single movie. Plus biographies, interviews, profiles, and more. Over 560 pages! Hardcover only. Only a few of these left. $75.00

TREK HANDBOOK and TREK UNIVERSE
The Handbook offers a complete guide to conventions, clubs, fanzines.
The Universe presents a complete guide to every book, comic, record and everything else.
Both volumes are edited by Enterprise Incidents editor James Van Hise. Join a universe of Trek fun!
Handbook...$12.95   Universe...$17.95

THE CREW BOOK
The crew of the Enterprise including coverage of Kirk, Spock, McCoy, Scotty, Uhura,Chekov, Sulu and all the others...plus starship staffing practices...250 pages...$17.95

THE MAKING OF THE NEXT GENERATION: SCRIPT TO SCREEN
THIS BOOK WILL NOT BE PRINTED UNTIL APRIL OR MAY. Analysis of every episode in each stage, from initial draft to final filmed script. Includes interviews with the writers and directors. 240 pages...$14.95

THE COUCH POTATO BOOK CATALOG 5715 N BALSAM, LAS VEGAS, NV 89130

THE FREDDY KRUEGER STORY
The making of the monster. Including interviews with director Wes Craven and star Robert Englund. Plus an interview with Freddy himself! $14.95

THE ALIENS STORY
Interviews with movie director James Cameron, stars Sigourney Weaver and Michael Biehn and effects people and designers Ron Cobb, Syd Mead, Doug Beswick and lots more!...$14.95

ROBOCOP
Law enforcement in the future. Includes interviews with the stars, the director, the writer, the special effects people, the storyboard artists and the makeup men! $16.95

MONSTERLAND'S HORROR IN THE '80s
The definitive book of the horror films of the '80s. Includes interviews with the stars and makers of Aliens, Freddy Krueger, Robocop, Predator, Fright Night, Terminator and all the others! $17.95

LOST IN SPACE

THE COMPLEAT LOST IN SPACE
244 PAGES...$17.95
TRIBUTE BOOK
Interviews with everyone!...$7.95
TECH MANUAL
Technical diagrams to all of the special ships and devices plus exclusive production artwork....$9.95

GERRY ANDERSON

SUPERMARIONATION
Episode guides and character profiles to Capt Scarlet, Stingray, Fireball, Thunderbirds, Supercar and more...240 pages...$17.95

BEAUTY AND THE BEAST

THE UNOFFICIAL BEAUTY & BEAST
Complete first season guide including interviews and biographies of the stars.
132 pages
$14.95

DARK SHADOWS

DARK SHADOWS TRIBUTE BOOK
Interviews, scripts and more...
160 pages...$14.95

DARK SHADOWS INTERVIEWS BOOK
A special book interviewing the entire cast.
$18.95

DOCTOR WHO THE BAKER YEARS
A complete guide to Tom Baker's seasons as the Doctor including an in-depth episode guide, interviews with the companions and profiles of the characters...
300 pages...$19.95

THE DOCTOR WHO ENCYCLOPEDIA: THE FOURTH DOCTOR
Encyclopedia of every character, villain and monster of the Baker Years.
..240 pages...$19.95

Boring, but Necessary Ordering Information!

Payment: All orders must be prepaid by check or money order. Do not send cash. All payments must be made in US funds only.

Shipping: We offer several methods of shipment for our product.

Postage is as follows:

For books priced under $10.00— for the first book add $2.50. For each additional book under $10.00 add $1.00. (This is per individual book priced under $10.00, not the order total.)

For books priced over $10.00— for the first book add $3.25. For each additional book over $10.00 add $2.00. (This is per individual book priced over $10.00, not the order total.)

These orders are filled as quickly as possible. Sometimes a book can be delayed if we are temporarily out of stock. You should note on your order whether you prefer us to ship the book as soon as available or send you a merchandise credit good for other TV goodies or send you your money back immediately. Shipments normally take 2 or 3 weeks, but allow up to 12 weeks for delivery.

Special UPS 2 Day Blue Label RUSH SERVICE: Special service is available for desperate Couch Potatos. These books are shipped within 24 hours of when we receive your order and should take 2 days to get from us to you.

For the first **RUSH SERVICE** book under $10.00 add $4.00. For each additional 1 book under $10.00 and $1.25. (This is per individual book priced under $10.00, not the order total.)

For the first **RUSH SERVICE** book over $10.00 add $6.00. For each additional book over $10.00 add $3.50 per book. (This is per individual book priced over $10.00, not the order total.)

Canadian and Foreign shipping rates are the same except that Blue Label RUSH SERVICE is not available. All Canadian and Foreign orders are shipped as books or printed matter.

DISCOUNTS! DISCOUNTS! Because your orders are what keep us in business we offer a discount to people that buy a lot of our books as our way of saying thanks. On orders over $25.00 we give a 5% discount. On orders over $50.00 we give a 10% discount. On orders over $100.00 we give a 15% discount. On orders over $150.00 we give a 20% discount. Please list alternates when possible. Please state if you wish a refund or for us to backorder an item if it is not in stock.

100% satisfaction guaranteed. We value your support. You will receive a full refund as long as the copy of the book you are not happy with is received back by us in reasonable condition. No questions asked, except we would like to know how we failed you. Refunds and credits are given as soon as we receive back the item you do not want.

Please have mercy on Phyllis and carefully fill out this form in the neatest way you can. Remember, she has to read a lot of them every day and she wants to get it right and keep you happy! You may use a duplicate of this order blank as long as it is clear. **Please don't forget to include payment! And remember, we *love* repeat friends...**

■■■■■■■■■■■■■■■■■■■■■■■■■■<u>ORDER FORM</u>■■■■■■■■■■■■■■■■■■■■■■■■■■■

_____The Phantom $16.95
_____The Green Hornet $16.95
_____The Shadow $16.95
_____Flash Gordon Part One $16.95_____Part Two $16.95
_____Blackhawk $16.95
_____Batman $16.95
_____The UNCLE Technical Manual One $9.95 _____Two $9.95
_____The Green Hornet Television Book $14.95
_____Number Six The Prisoner Book $14.95
_____The Wild Wild West $17.95
_____Trek Year One $10.95
_____Trek Year Two $12.95
_____Trek Year Three $12.95
_____The Animated Trek $14.95
_____The Movies $12.95
_____Next Generation $19.95
_____The Lost Years $14.95
_____The Trek Encyclopedia $19.95
_____Interviews Aboard The Enterprise $18.95
_____The Ultimate Trek $75.00
_____Trek Handbook $12.95_____Trek Universe $17.95
_____The Crew Book $17.95
_____The Making of the Next Generation $14.95
_____The Freddy Krueger Story $14.95
_____The Aliens Story $14.95
_____Robocop $16.95
_____Monsterland's Horror in the '80s $17.95
_____The Compleat Lost in Space $17.95
_____Lost in Space Tribute Book $9.95
_____Lost in Space Tech Manual $9.95
_____Supermarionation $17.95
_____The Unofficial Beauty and the Beast $14.95
_____Dark Shadows Tribute Book $14.95
_____Dark Shadows Interview Book $18.95
_____Doctor Who Baker Years $19.95
_____The Doctor Who Encyclopedia:The 4th Doctor $19.95
_____Illustrated Stephen King $12.95
_____Gunsmoke Years $14.95

NAME:_____

STREET:_____

CITY:_____

STATE:_____

ZIP:_____

TOTAL:_____ SHIPPING_____

**SEND TO: COUCH POTATO,INC.
5715 N BALSAM, LAS VEGAS, NV 89130**